AUTUMN IN SYCAMORE PARK

CP WARD

AMMFA
PUBLISHING

AUTUMN IN SYCAMORE PARK

For Eriko,

may your autumn be long
and filled with colour

AUTUMN IN SYCAMORE PARK

1

A NEW WIND BLOWING

ANIMALS.

With her front foot nudging the base of the fire doors, and the hand not clutching the overloaded bag of textbooks she might or might not need lifted in readiness to force her way ahead, Jennifer Stevens paused at the entrance to Brentwell Primary, racked by a sudden tsunami of self-doubt.

Imagine them as blood-thirsty, cannibalistic animals, and things couldn't surely go worse. In fact, things might seem better.

Another voice was more practical: *think of the rent, the electricity, and the hot water you're going to need if we get the kind of winter the TV keeps talking about. You need this job, and you've got this.*

And still a third had something to say, making Jennifer wonder just how many of them there might be knocking about up there, waiting to show themselves at the exact wrong moment and get her committed, or worse: *run, while you still can. Buy that camper van that you've always promised yourself and take off across Europe. You're thirty-six,*

Jennifer, remember? The clock is ticking. Most people your age are married off and/or dragging balls and chains in the shape of the little darlings you get to wave goodbye to at a quarter past three each day. Be thankful for your holy singleness. You nearly screwed it up in Dottenham. Don't make the same mistake again. Are you paying attention?

She was, at least she had thought so until the door in front of her began to open with a sudden alarming creak of its hinges. Slowed in its outward arc by a fireproof mat, the delay was just long enough for Jennifer to step backwards onto a patch of muddy grass before a paper cup of coffee, closely followed by an arm in a navy blue sweater, and then finally by the remainder of a human male a little younger than Jennifer, stepped outside.

He made straight for the steps she had so recently vacated, and might have passed her by without acknowledgement, had she not slipped in a little patch of mud and, afraid of unbalancing, let out a gasp of fright. Pausing in his stride, he glanced sideways, his face registering a hint of both surprise and shock, followed by a rather inappropriately raised eyebrow. He was easy enough on the eye, if a little young for Jennifer's tastes, but an annoyed smirk doused any potential fire of excitement before it could really get going.

'Oh, hello,' he said, the condescension in his voice matching that in his face. 'Are you the new girl?'

'Um, thank you for not showering me with coffee. I was just considering quitting before I'd even started, but you've made me strengthen my resolve just enough to at least make it as far as the staffroom.' She stuck out a hand. 'Jennifer Stevens.'

'Rick Fellow. I teach Year Five. You replaced Clara Goldsmith, is that right?'

'I don't know her name, only that she retired.'

Rick nodded. 'All good, then. Her class are the angels. You'll be fine.'

'Please tell me you're not just saying that.'

'No, I'm not. Actually, yes I am. They're a nightmare. They told you she retired, but that was a lie because they couldn't get anyone to take the job. She's in a mental institution, straitjacketed, night and day. Apparently she wails all night long about pins being left on her chair, and buckets of water propped over a slightly ajar door.'

Jennifer stared. Rick started to laugh, one hand on a metal handrail, the other barely keeping hold of the coffee.

'Sorry, I really am joking. They're all right, your lot. Actually, they're so quiet they have a ready made nickname this year … the Year Trees. Old Clara could barely get a word out of them. Said those classes dragged. Probably why she was lacing her coffee with brandy of a Monday morning.'

'That's it,' Jennifer said. 'I quit.'

She started to turn, but her heel chose that moment to slip in the mud, and to stop herself falling, she snatched for the handrail by the steps, managing only to grab hold of Rick's hand.

A moment of awkwardness passed between them before Jennifer steadied herself and regained the safety of the concrete footpath.

'Careful, if the kids see us there'll be talk,' Rick said, with another smug grin. 'Anyway, it was lovely to meet you. I hope to see you again before you run screaming from this place with your tail between your legs. I left something in my car, so I'd better get a move on.'

He hurried on down the footpath, leaving Jennifer standing by the door. She smoothed down her blouse and jacket, then headed inside, along the corridor, following signs for a reception desk. At least now she'd broken the ice with one member of staff, she felt a little better, even if Rick Fellow hadn't left the best impression. She passed a few groups of children in sky-blue sweaters and black trousers and skirts, all of whom treated her as though she didn't exist. She glanced across a few faces, wondering which, if any, might be in her class.

'Hello?' she called into the reception window. 'I'm Jennifer Stevens. The new Year Three form teacher?'

A dumpy woman in her fifties who looked like she hadn't smiled since childhood, dropped down a pile of photocopying with a sigh and came stumping over.

'Yes?'

'Jennifer Stevens?'

'What? I'm Maud Lee. What can I help you with?'

'Uh, no, I mean that I'm Jennifer Stevens. The new teacher?'

'Ah. You're the one who couldn't make the training days.'

'I was moving house—'

'Hang on a minute. I'll call the Head. He's in the morning meeting.'

Jennifer, feeling more and more awkward as the minutes passed, waited for the headmaster to arrive. A few more groups of kids passed her as they ambled towards class. Some of them sniggered behind cupped hands, making Jennifer tingle with the first rattle of paranoia.

Please don't be like Dottenham. Please, please, please.

A stern man in a grey sweater vest over a greyer Marks & Spencer shirt stepped out of a door a little further down the corridor. His hair was pepper flecked and thinning down a centre line. Just like the receptionist, he looked unfamiliar to the concept of happiness, and couldn't have been more of a headmaster stereotype if Jennifer had cut him out of a school prospectus. Jennifer smiled as he glared at her, eyes narrowing behind thin-rimmed glasses, nostrils flaring like a bull readying for a charge.

'Miss Stevens?'

'Yes, that's me.'

With a sudden unexpected grin, the man clapped his hands together and gave a hearty laugh.

'You're young! They're going to love you.'

'Excuse me? I'm thirty-six—'

'Have you been a teacher long? You can't have been. They say teachers age at twice the rate of normal people.' Before Jennifer could point out that she had only been a teacher for three years, having opted for a career change after years of boring office work, but that it had been three of the hardest years of her life, the man stuck out a hand and said, 'Greg Downton. Call me Greg in private, Mr. Downton in front of the kids.'

He led her down the corridor and into a messy, busy staffroom. Calling for a moment's attention from the other assembled teachers, none of whom looked willing to stop what they were doing, he introduced her.

'Pay attention please, we're supposed to be in a meeting, remember?' When no one responded other than to close books or set coffees down, he raised his voice a level and said, 'This is Jennifer Stevens.' From behind a photocopier near the back, Rick Fellow gave her a little wave. 'She's the new form teacher for Year Three. As you know, she couldn't make the training days, so please lend her a hand if need be. Do you want to say anything, Jennifer?'

Caught off guard, Jennifer just stared at the faces watching her. Aside from Rick and one tubby young girl who gave her a wide grin, most of the teachers were older than her and looked keen to get back on with their work.

'Uh, it's nice to meet you,' Jennifer stammered. 'I'm looking forward to working here.'

One teacher near the front, a short man with an obvious comb-over, snorted and said something under his breath as he rifled through a stack of papers. Another older woman sighed.

'Right, well, that's nice,' Greg Downton said. 'Enjoy your day, everyone. Oh, by the way, Colin Waite from Year Four got caught shoplifting last night and has been suspended for a week. He bagged the new edition of Resident Evil from Kay's Electrics on the high street.'

'Good game, that,' Rick said, at the same time as the short teacher in the front muttered, 'Send the thug to Borstal.'

'Yes, well, can you gather after lunch for a short meeting about it?' As several teachers moaned under their breath, Greg seemed to remember Jennifer was standing beside him. 'Oh, your desk is back there, between Miss Clairmont and Mr. Fellow. I'm sure they'll show you how it all works. Come to my office at nine-fifteen and I'll take you to your class. I'm sure the little toerags are looking forward to meeting you.'

Jennifer grimaced. 'I hope so,' she said.

2

SYCAMORE PARK

GREG DOWNTON LOOKED around the watching faces. 'Stand up, please.'

The twenty children sitting around five bright blue plastic desks all stood up. A couple at the back pushed each other, one other dithering girl wanted to finish off a doodle Jennifer hoped was supposed to be Snoopy on her notebook. Greg clapped his hands sharply, and at last the class stood to attention.

'This is Miss Stevens,' Greg said. 'She will be your teacher in Year Three. Call her Miss Stevens, and be polite, or you'll be outside my office or picking up leaves from the school field every lunchtime. Is that understood?'

A chorus of muted 'Yes, sirs,' came from the children.

'Good.' Greg clapped his hands together again. 'Right, well, it's over to you, Jen—uh, Miss Stevens. Don't let these ... *darlings* fool you with their innocence. Any dissent and you send them straight to me.'

Jennifer gave Greg an awkward nod as the stern headmaster went out, closing the door with a loud thump. She looked around the kids, most of whom were still staring at her, feeling a sudden brain-freeze. She'd survived for three years in Dottenham, and while at times that school had been a living hell, the kids alone hadn't been the reason why she'd left.

A hand had risen from a short, frail boy with spectacles so thick you couldn't be sure of the size of his eyes.

'Ah, yes? What's your name?'

'Matthew Bridges,' the boy said, in a weak, nervous voice.

'Yes, Matthew, do you have a question?'

'Yes, Miss. Is Miss Goldsmith coming back?'

The rest of the class erupted into sudden cheers, the boys clapping each other on the backs, the girls tittering behind their hands. One rough-looking boy gave Matthew a hearty back slap, to which the boy just looked down at his feet, and Jennifer got the impression she had been the butt of a joke the poor boy had been set up to deliver.

'I'm afraid she's never coming back,' she said, feeling a sudden resentment towards this group of devils in Tesco Back-to-School clothing. 'She's never coming back again. In fact—'

Don't say it, don't say it, whispered a voice of reason that Jennifer was quick to stamp out.

'—she's never coming back, because she's joined a cult and run off to South America.'

A little girl at the back began to cry, and Jennifer immediately felt like the worst teacher in the world. She smiled, clapping her hands together, and said, 'That was a joke! She's fine … as far as I know. She's just retired. It happens. You'll retire one day, when you're old and grey.'

Two girls were now crying.

Near the front, a tall boy with a sensible, mature look in his eyes leaned forward and whispered, 'Miss, first class is geography. Why don't we watch a DVD?'

Jennifer was tempted to berate him for trying to do her job, but as he nodded at a box of DVDs next to a large, widescreen TV in the corner, she understood.

He was trying to save her.

'Great idea,' she said, hurrying across to the box and pulling out a documentary on Ancient Egypt. It wasn't geography, but what did it matter? They probably didn't know the difference ... or so she hoped. 'Get your notebooks out, please.'

Her hands were shaking as she slid the DVD into the player, and to her relief the disc automatically started to play. The sensible boy, along with two others, jumped up and began to run around the classroom, closing the curtains, while the other kids shuffled their chairs forward.

As another boy switched off the lights, Jennifer sat down on a stool in the semi-darkness and breathed a sigh of relief.

She could do this. She really could.

And she didn't need a swift glass of wine to pull it off.

By LUNCH TIME, things had begun to take a turn for the better. After half an hour of watching the DVD on Ancient Egypt, she'd set them to drawing pictures of Egyptians in extravagant, scribbled headdresses, which took the focus off her long enough that she could begin to get herself together. With the kids busy in their activity, she was able to mingle, learn a few names, pick up on some of the class dynamics.

Matthew Bridges was the class whipping boy, the butt of all the jokes, the poor kid whose very appearance made school life a never-ending minefield. The kid sitting next to him, Gavin Gordon, the resident disrupter and bully, had seemingly altered his seating position after Miss Gold-smith's departure, hoping Jennifer wouldn't notice. Quickly picking up on the vibe, however, she moved him to sit further to the back, among a group of bigger boys less likely to put up with his teasing, and giving Matthew—during class time at least—a little respite.

Overall, though, they seemed like nice kids. With the exception of Gavin and a couple of other rowdy boys, they were polite, called her Miss, and didn't give her much backtalk. There were a pair of identical twins—Becky and Kelly Jarder—whom she couldn't yet tell apart, but other-wise, she was surviving with at least tentative ease.

'You made it to lunchtime without handing in your papers,' said Miss Clairmont, standing by the door to the dining hall, a Paw Patrol apron tied around her waist. One of the dogs—Jennifer couldn't guess at their names—had its eyes obscured by some old scorch mark. 'It's tough when you're starting at a new school, isn't it?'

Jennifer smiled. 'It's a work in progress,' she said.

'Miss Goldsmith had them from Reception to Year Two, and kids always bond with their first teacher. I'm Amy, by the way. Of course, you have to call me Miss Clairmont in front of the kids, otherwise Old Downton Abbey will have a fit.'

'Is that his nickname?'

Amy glanced from side to side and smiled. 'I didn't tell you,' she said. 'The kids were straight on it a few years back when the show came out. The first kid to say it to his face got suspended, so it went underground. Now the show's finished, it's died out among the kids for the most part, but us teachers have longer memories.'

'He's certainly a little stern.'

'You'll get used to it.'

'If I survive long enough.'

Amy smiled. 'I'd worry more about Rick than the kids.'

'Rick? You mean, uh, Mr. Fellow?'

'Our resident conquistador. You're single, aren't you?'

'Ah—'

'At least, there's nothing on your finger. Mind you, if there was, he'd see it as a challenge.'

Jennifer was still struggling over how to respond when Amy shrugged. 'Oh well. Time to get this next herd to the feeding troughs. Speak to you later.'

AFTER HAVING to break up a playground fight just after lunch, and then enduring a chaotic art class in sixth period when Gavin Gordon poured a pot of black paint over Matthew's painting of sunflowers, causing the smaller boy to burst into tears, Jennifer was glad to hear the final bell and wave her children off for the day. She had anticipated having to stay late to deal with any emergency stuff that came up or report her progress to Greg, but the head-master was out on business, while Rick had gone home early, allowing her to clear up and arrange some things for tomorrow without hassle. She shared a quick cup of tea with Amy, then headed back to her new flat at just after five p.m.

The threat of rain that had lingered most of the day had cleared up, leaving a beautiful, clear, afternoon sky to accompany her as she walked up the high street and past a Tesco Metro, where she grabbed something for dinner. As she climbed the stairs to her second floor flat, she paused, gave a little smile, and then knocked on the door.

A scrabble of paws came from inside, followed by a tirade of excited yapping. She opened the door and Bonky, her little toy poodle, practically jumped into her arms, before encircling her with a series of rapid turns, his little tail wagging frantically.

'Right,' she said, scooping the dog up and carrying him back into the flat, where many of her boxes still stood waiting to be unpacked. From his bed by the living room window, her cat, James, looked up, gave her a brief miaow as though to remind her of his existence, then resumed watching whatever was going on outside.

With Bonky still tucked under her arm, Jennifer scooted around the mess of her personal life, delivering tonight's dinner to the narrow kitchen tacked on to the side of the slightly bigger living room, wishing she'd spent more time browsing for flats before deciding on this one. Honestly, though, it had looked a lot bigger in the pictures, and at least she could afford it. Even for a small town like Brentwell, the local rents were staggeringly high for a relative beginner teacher to afford.

To her frustration, she had forgotten to turn the fridge on, which meant the milk had gone sour. The margarine and the half finished tin of pasta sauce from yesterday would survive, but she had been dreaming of a coffee on her only chair all the way home. Still, she had passed a Spar on the way, and Bonky needed his walk, so she could pick up some milk on the way back.

Moving a couple of boxes aside, she fed a delighted Bonky, while James ambled over to nudge the vibrating dog aside and take his share. Then, giving her cat a quick, mostly ignored rub, Jennifer hunted out the dog's lead from a box and pulled her jacket back on.

'Walkies,' she said, to which the little dog began to yap and spin in circles. James gave both of them a nonchalant glance before returning to his bed.

The day's warmth still lingered as Jennifer urged the little dog along the edge of the pavement, Bonky content to inspect every patch of grass, litter bin, or lamp post. Having rattled through her late arrival yesterday and her frantic first day at work, Jennifer hadn't had a chance to explore her new home. Now, with Bonky taking his time, she got to really look at her little suburb of Brentwell for the first time.

Her road, Willis Lane, was a long, meandering suburban street which connected at one end to the high street, and at the other to an industrial estate. Several other roads intersected with it, heading north and south, but until now Jennifer hadn't had a chance to have a look at them. To the south, the houses were larger, detached buildings with neat front lawns. North, towards the old town centre, the houses were taller, Georgian and Edwardian terraces, most separated into flats or turned into offices for lawyers, accountants, and financial consultants. They looked very much alike, but as she reached a junction with a road called Sycamore Place, she noticed a stand of trees at the far end surrounding the entrance to a park.

'That looks a bit more interesting than your lamp post,' she said to Bonky, as he cocked his leg over a patch of weeds. 'Let's go.'

It took about ten minutes to coax the dog to the entrance of the park, but as she stepped through a pair of open cast iron gates, Jennifer couldn't help but smile at the sign attached to one.

Welcome to Sycamore Park

Tarmac footpaths curved away to the right and left, beneath towering sycamore, oak, and beech trees. In front of her was a gentle grassy slope leading up to a rock feature at its peak. Through the trees to the right she spotted a children's play area. To the left, a duck pond surrounded by benches. A signpost told her that to the north was the public library, to the west, the town theatre.

The sun, low in the sky, was glittering through the branches of the trees. A light, tickling breeze blew, making the leaves rustle. Jennifer gave a contented smile, as all her frustrations melted away. As another dog walker gave her a polite smile and said 'Good evening,' Jennifer smiled back, then reached down and patted Bonky.

'Well, look what treasure we've found,' she said.

3

OAK LEAF CAFÉ

ACCORDING to a sign by the entrance, dogs under a certain size were free to be let off their leads, so Jennifer unclipped Bonky's harness and let him rush off on a pigeon hunt. Jennifer ambled slowly after him, enjoying the cool tickle of the breeze on her face, and the occasional warmth of the evening sun as it caught her through the trees.

With a couple of hours of daylight left, Sycamore Park was quite busy. Several young mothers stood talking by the play area while their preschool-aged children clambered on the climbing frames and played on the swings and slides. Several other dog walkers wandered along a series of smaller paths off the main circular one, or chased their dogs across the grassy field. A young couple walked arm in arm. A couple of old men sat on a bench near the duck pond, talking quietly. On a paved courtyard outside the theatre, a group of students appeared to be rehearsing for a play.

With a gruff bark, Bonky caught sight of a pigeon seemingly up for the challenge, and raced in pursuit up the grassy slope towards the rock feature. Jennifer followed, catching up with the dog near the top as he paused to regard the pigeon, now perched out of reach on one of the large stones laid around in a rough circle. It cooed once at the dog, then flapped off to the branches of a nearby tree.

Jennifer sat down on one of the stones. From here you could see the whole park. The main walking path made a complete circle, with numerous other pathways leading to monuments or secluded play areas. To the south and east, the surrounding streets were residential, with the thickest patch of trees and the theatre over to the west. To the north, a small car park stood beside the library, a two-storey Georgian building. Outside were a newspaper stand and a couple of other stalls, now closed. Down a small, tree-lined side road on the library's right, tables and chairs were set out on a pedestrian-only street, a signboard Jennifer couldn't read at this distance standing among them.

'Shall we go and take a look?' Jennifer said to the little dog, who had sat down on the grass and was watching her, tongue lolling. 'Might be a bit more interesting than dinner out of a plastic packet. Do you think James will mind?'

The dog gave her a little bark and wagged his tail. Of course the cat wouldn't mind.

'Let's go, then.'

She attached Bonky's harness again and headed down the slope. The library was closed—at six p.m., a sign on the door said—but the little café appeared to be open, even though no one was sitting outside. Jennifer paused, looking at the sign over the door.

Oak Leaf Café.

The front was wood paneled with the name carved into a larger piece over the door. The tables were also wooden, and while Jennifer suspected they were pine rather than oak, each had a little vase of autumn twigs and leaves in the centre, adding to the quaintness. Next to a triangular menu, salt and pepper pots were also made out of wood.

'What do you think?' she said to the little dog, who appeared insistent on inspecting each chair leg in turn. 'Although, it's a little chilly.'

'Feel free to bring the little guy inside,' came a voice from the doorway, and Jennifer looked up to see a middle-aged woman leaning on the door frame, wearing a maple leaf-designed apron over jeans and a white t-shirt. Grey-flecked light brown hair was tied back into a ponytail. Bright green eyes sparkled through the glasses she wore, and a face that still retained a hint of youthful beauty gave Jennifer a warm smile.

'Oh, would that be all right?'

The woman waved. 'Sure. I've even got some food out the back somewhere if he's hungry.'

'Well, thank you.'

'Come in and have a look at the menu if you're interested. I love the wind off the park in this season, but it gets a little chilly once the sun goes behind the theatre.'

Jennifer went into a pretty, wood-panelled interior. Six wooden tables stood neatly arranged in front of a counter-top. In little nooks and alcoves, pots of dried flowers stood, giving off a gentle lavender aroma. On the wall, framed posters identified various varieties of pumpkins and squashes. Antique cooking pots and utensils lined shelves in front of the windows delicately framed with lace curtains.

One table by the window had a view of Sycamore Park. 'That one,' Jennifer said. 'I'd like to sit there, please.'

'Take your pick,' the woman said. 'We're not exactly bursting at the seams.' She smiled again. 'My name is Angela. Angela Dawson. With only the two of us here, I don't think it would be proper to remain strangers, would it?'

'I suppose not. I'm Jennifer. Jennifer Stevens. I just moved to Brentwell. Yesterday, actually. I work at the local primary. Today was my first day.'

'Busy times! I don't know how you young people handle it. I get tired just walking around the park in the morning. And who's this little guy?'

Angela bent down to pet Bonky, who lapped up the attention with a frantic wag of his tail.

'Ah, his name is Bonky. He's two years old.'

'I had a toy poodle as a child, many, many years ago. Lovely little things.' Angela stood up. 'Bonky? That's … interesting.'

For the first year or so, Jennifer had always felt a flush off embarrassment telling people the name of her dog, but she had got used to it. After all, it was just a name, albeit a little unusual.

'Yeah, the kids at my old school chose it. I was having a few issues with some of them, and I thought getting them to choose the name for my dog would be a form of bonding. I was expecting something generic like Harry or Rover, but … nope. Bonky. They came up with Bonky.' She shrugged. 'And so it stuck.'

'Well, it's kind of cute, isn't it?'

'I suppose.'

'Is that why you came to Brentwell? Because you were having problems at your old school?'

Jennifer might have expected the question from Rick or Amy or one of the other teachers, but due to the new-term rush she'd so far avoided it. Hearing it from Angela had caught her off guard, and she stared at the older lady openmouthed, then gave a little shake of her head.

'Uh, that's not all of it.'

Angela gave a shrug. 'I'm sorry, I was prying. How about we sort you out with something to eat. There's a menu there, but I'm afraid we're out of season so you're stuck with whatever I've got cooking. Today's special is cheese, apple, and potato pie with homemade gravy, seasonal vegetables, and fried pear fritters for desert. Would that do?'

Jennifer stared. She thought about the meagre supplies back at her flat and gave a slow nod.

'That would be just great. In fact, it would be more than great.'

'Excellent. Coming right up.'

Angela disappeared into a kitchen behind the counter, and soon delightful smells began to waft through, reminding Jennifer that she hadn't eaten anything since a sandwich at lunchtime. Bonky settled down at her feet, and Jennifer picked a home décor magazine off a nearby rack and began to browse through picturesque designs of autumn-themed homes and gardens. Even before Angela reappeared with a large plate loaded with steaming pie and vegetables, the day's traumas already felt resolved and compartmentalised. Tomorrow was a new day, as they said.

'Well, here you are.'

'I'm not sure I can eat all that,' Jennifer said with a smile, even though she fully planned to try.

'Actually, I want to bake another in the morning, so I tried to give you all that was left. I couldn't quite fit it on the plate, so I've put it in a Tupperware for you to take home. That's if you like it, of course. If you don't, not to worry. Just pass it on to a neighbour.'

'I haven't met mine yet. In fact, I haven't actually unpacked yet either.'

Angela waved a hand. 'There's always tomorrow. Anyway, you enjoy your meal. I'll just bring a little something for Bonky, plus perhaps a cushion. The floor might be a little hard.'

Angela started to walk away, but Jennifer put up a hand and muttered, 'Uh, excuse me…?' in a way that reminded her of some of the more shy members of her class.

'Yes?'

'Um, if you haven't eaten, would you like to join me?' Jennifer shrugged. 'Bonky isn't the best for conversation, particularly when he's tired. Chasing all those pigeons, you know….'

Angela looked at her a moment, then shrugged. 'Well, sure. If you'll indulge me a little. You walked here, didn't you?'

'Yes.'

'Perfect.'

Angela went back into the kitchen, then returned a moment later with a bottle of wine and two glasses.

'Chilean Red,' she said, holding up the bottle. 'Perfect for an autumn evening.' She winked. 'It's a little chilly, and the skies are red … sorry, that's a shocker.'

It took Jennifer a moment to catch the attempted joke, but when she did, she gave a sympathetic laugh. 'I've heard worse. And far ruder, too.'

'Well, let's drink to autumn, to long, cool evenings, and to new friends.'

Almost to signal his agreement, Bonky looked up and gave a sharp bark.

Jennifer took the offered glass and smiled. 'I'll drink to that,' she said.

4

BIG GERRY

ANGELA DAWSON PROVED ENLIGHTENING and entertaining company. Jennifer still had a smile on her face the next morning when she woke up, surrounded by piles of unpacked boxes. Bonky was in his basket beside the bed, and James was curled up between her feet. Dawn light was streaming through a window she had not yet had time to hang with curtains, and the alarm clock on her bedside table read 6.45 a.m.

Bonky, as astute as ever, immediately noticed Jennifer was awake, and began to make a fuss. She hauled herself out of bed, got herself ready for work, fed a lethargic James, then grabbed Bonky's lead and together they headed out for his morning walk.

At just after seven, the street lights were still on even though the sky was beginning to lighten in the east. With not a cloud in the sky it looked like the beginning of another beautiful autumn day, even if the air was chilly enough to make Jennifer thankful for her jacket.

The streets were empty besides a couple of morning joggers and dog walkers. Jennifer wandered down Willis

Lane to the junction with Sycamore Place. At the far end, the gates to Sycamore Park stood open in the gloom.

Bonky seemed keen to go that way.

'Okay, why not?'

Jennifer led the dog up to the park. Under the trees it was mostly dark, but street lights along the park's paths gave enough light for the joggers and dog walkers to navigate by. She took Bonky over to the duck pond, where a number of birds sat around the water, their heads tucked under their wings. She kept the dog on his lead so as not to disturb them, but Bonky was happy enough to inspect the bushes instead.

They did a quick circuit of the park. When they passed the Oak Leaf Café, Jennifer looked up at the windows, but they were still dark. Angela, all laughter and tall tales, had kept her longer than she had planned, until way after the café's official closing time. A sign on the door said that it opened for breakfast at eight, so with a wry smile, Jennifer hoped Angela made it.

Back at the house half an hour later, she grabbed her school things and headed out. The thought of work put an immediate dampener on everything, but at least she could look forward to a walk in the park after work, especially if the skies stayed clear. As she walked up Willis Lane to the high street, she felt better than she had at any time since her rushed and abrupt departure from Dottingham.

She had just turned off the high street on to Clover Drive, which led up to Brentwell Primary, when she spotted little Matthew Bridges walking on his own on the other side of the street, his head bowed, bag slung almost low enough to touch the ground. One of the boy's shoelaces was untied, and dragged along the pavement behind his shoe. His shirt was untucked at the back, poking out of his school sweater like the corner of an envelope.

'Matthew! Good morning!' she called, lifting a hand to wave as he glanced back. He caught her eye, gave a half nod, then carried on his way.

Labels began to offer themselves, but it was too early to make any kind of a judgment on the boy or his home life. Getting involved with problem families had been something Jennifer hadn't anticipated during her first teaching job. Looking back on it, she couldn't decide which was worse, the kids living below the breadline or the ones so far above it they no longer had a grounding in reality.

As she was walking across the teachers' car park, a shiny BMW roared into a spot just in front of her and came to a lurching stop with an angry squeal of brakes. Jennifer hurried past before it could reverse into her, but before she had reached the teachers' entrance Rick Fellow's voice came from behind her.

'Hey, there you are.'

She tried to get inside before he could catch up, but the bag she was carrying slowed her down.

'Let me get that.'

'I can manage.'

'Sure you can. Newbie problem, that, eh? Getting a door open with your toe while carrying a pile of marking? A skill every teacher needs.'

'Well, thanks,' Jennifer said, as he pulled the door back for her, giving her a gusting whiff of expensive aftershave, mingled with the more pleasant scent from the plastic cup of coffee he was holding in his other hand.

'You know, I saw you walking up the hill,' he said. 'If you don't have a car, perhaps we can pool.'

'Pool?'

'Yeah. I'll pick you up in the mornings, drop you home again. If you like.'

'I only live a mile from the school.'

'But you don't want the kids knowing your address, do you? Damn animals, the lot of them. You'll open the door in the morning to find a bunch of them on the steps outside, wanting you to throw them some scraps.'

Jennifer shrugged. 'I doubt they'd care. I'm not a celebrity.'

'You are to them. They'll want to know everything. What you eat for dinner, boyfriends.'

'Just those two specific things? The answer would be whatever I feel like and none.'

She had meant it as a hard brush off, but the moment the last word left her lips, she realised her mistake. It wasn't the kids hounding her that she would have to worry about.

'Is that so?'

'And I'm not looking, either.'

Rick gave a sorrowful expression. 'Did someone break your heart?'

'Look, I've got stuff to do before class.'

'Sure.'

She headed inside, Rick trailing along behind. Only when she reached the staffroom was she able to dilute him among the others. Amy Clairmont was already at her desk, arranging a box of pencil crayons into colour groups.

'So, you came back?' Amy grinned. 'I owe Bob over there a couple of quid.'

'What?'

'I'm joking. Are you ready to jump back in again?'

'Head first.'

Amy gave a polite chuckle. 'That's the spirit.'

THE DAY PASSED with relative calm until P.E. in sixth period when Kelly Garder slipped during an indoor game of rounders and her plimsoll came off. Swooping like a hawk, Gavin Gordon grabbed it off the floor and chucked it into the back of the alcove space in which all the folding dinner tables and chairs were stacked. After sending Gavin to Greg Downton's office, Jennifer was required to climb into the hell of jutting, dust-covered chair and table legs in order to retrieve it. By the time she had managed to get back out, the bell had rung and the kids were late for the school bus. Three kids, terrified of having to walk home, were crying, while three others had already run off early, requiring Jennifer to run out to the car park just in case they got on the wrong bus.

As she waved the last child off onto the bus and ticked the name off on her registration sheet, she let out a sigh of relief, already dreaming of getting home to her pets. Plus, it was a nice afternoon, so a stroll in Sycamore Park would make her feel better. She might even stop by at the Oak Leaf Café to see what Angela was cooking.

She met Greg back in the staffroom. 'Sent the little sod home with a note to his parents,' he said. 'Whether it gets there or not, I don't know. I could have Maud give them a call tomorrow. Not that it'll make much difference. The boy's heading for the slammer. Might as well lock him up now and get on with it.'

Jennifer wasn't sure what to say. She was still formulating a reply when Greg turned to deal with another issue, so she headed back to her desk. At the desk beside her, Amy was emptying poster glue out of one large industrial pot into a couple of dozen smaller ones, measuring the depths with a ruler, frowning whenever a little spilled.

'Did the Abbot give you his lowdown on which kid wouldn't make it?' she asked.

'The Abbot?'

Amy grinned. 'That's another one. There are a fair few

floating about. As before, you're sworn to lower level staff circle secrecy.'

'Got it. And to answer your question, yes, he mentioned one of my boys might be, um, prison-bound.'

'He does like his labels. 'Mine are only five and six years old, but according to Greg I've got the farmer, the pigeon racer/weirdo, the accountant, and the rocket scientist. A few are undecided, but by the time they get to Year Five he's pretty much got them all nailed down.'

Jennifer smiled. 'And it's our job to try to prove him wrong?'

Amy lifted a hand and clicked her fingers as though about to start up a jazz standard. A glob of poster glue landed on the front of Jennifer's schedule book, but she pretended not to notice.

'Exactly,' Amy said. 'Or at least we have to show them the options, make sure they know there are other paths to the one Father Super Ted has predicted for them.'

'Is, ah, that another one?'

'Huh? Oh, you mean Father … yes, that's right.'

Jennifer tapped the side of her nose. 'But it's a secret, right?'

'Ping-pong.'

BONKY, as ever, was delighted by Jennifer's return. She really wanted to spend some time unpacking, but the dog would not be denied his walk. The sun was peeking between the trees as she made her way down to Sycamore Park. She had brought a book with her from school, on best practices for teaching children, so she found a bench by the duck pond still warmed by a patch of sunlight, and let Bonky off his lead.

It was hard to concentrate on the book, though. Gazing out at the pond, watching the birds duck and dive, listening to the wind rustling the leaves … she felt like someone had inserted a straw into her head and was drawing out the stress of the teaching day. She closed her eyes and took a deep breath.

Three days in Brentwell, and she was beginning to think she had made the right choice. The agony of moving out of Mark's flat, quitting her job, suffering her parents' obvious disappointment … the doubts still shuddered through her, but they were less each day.

Bonky had run himself out chasing pigeons around the duck pond and came back to slump panting at Jennifer's feet. She reached down and scooped the dog up on to her lap, feeling the heat of his little body through the curls of fur.

'Are you ready for some dinner?'

When Jennifer reached Oak Leaf Café, she found Angela outside, squatting by one of the tables, fixing a bent table leg.

'Oh, hello,' Angela said, giving Jennifer a smile. 'How was the pie?'

'I was the envy of the staffroom,' Jennifer said. 'Ah, I forgot to bring your pot back. I'll drop it by tomorrow or on Saturday, if that's all right?'

'Any time is fine. I have dozens of the things. Can you hold this for me? It's been a bit wobbly for ages, and I need to give it a tweak. I had a customer nearly catapult a milkshake into their lap this afternoon. Wouldn't have been the best for business, although I'm pretty sure it was one of the local councillors, so perhaps its karma.' Angela gave her a wink. 'I see fewer bloodsuckers on Halloween.'

'What happened?'

Angela frowned. 'Well, the latest issue is that they want to chop down Big Gerry.'

'Who?'

Angela laughed. 'Not a who, but a what. You haven't seen Big Gerry yet? Come on, I'll show you.'

'What about the café?'

'Business isn't exactly booming. I'll put an "Out for Late Lunch" sign in the window in case anyone stops by. We'll only be a minute.'

'Do you usually eat lunch this late?'

Angela laughed. 'Lunch is an ongoing process from opening to closing,' she said. 'I couldn't let a customer's dish go out without having a nibble first, could I?'

Jennifer waited while Angela locked the café's front door, then together they headed into Sycamore Park. Angela took the path headed around to the east, then stopped in a shady, paved square which the roots of several surrounding trees had turned into lumpy, crazy paving.

'This was the old square before the newer one over by the theatre,' Angela said. 'As you can see, it's now great fun for kids, a nightmare for joggers. A hundred years or so ago when the park was built, these trees would have been a lot smaller.' She spread her arms. 'And this one over here is Big Gerry, the biggest of them all.'

In one corner of the old square, one sycamore tree dwarfed all the others. Three main limbs spread out from a single thick trunk, its circumference greater than half a dozen people holding hands. Its central limb rose skyward, its leaves so high Jennifer couldn't see the top through the canopy. The right-hand limb extended behind it over the grassy area in the park's corner, stretching out into a tree-climber's paradise of snaking branches. The left-hand limb extended out over the corner of the courtyard, but was angling slightly downwards, its droop caused by a crack near to its join with the main trunk.

Angela was beaming. 'The fourth oldest sycamore in England,' she said, her voice thick with pride. 'For all of us Sycamore Park regulars, he's a kind of god.'

'What happened to that damaged branch?'

Angela's smile dropped. 'A council crane reversed into it back in the spring when they were fixing a telephone cable. 'And now, with winter on the way, they're holding a vote on what to do with it. Apparently, erecting a support for the limb is too expensive, and the fear is that the tree is so old other bits might start to fall off.' Angela scoffed. 'Bah. As though that could happen. It's a tree, not a silly building.'

'So what are they going to do?'

Angela sighed. 'At the end of October they're going to cut down the whole thing.'

5

BAD NEWS

'HEY, how was your day? Tired enough that you'd be interested in a recovery drink tonight at a cocktail bar in town? A few of us are going.'

Jennifer stared at Rick until his smug grin finally dropped. 'Um, first, my day was fine, apart from Ben Jenner fainting in P.E. and then Gavin Gordon throwing a bowl of custard at Rachel Low at lunchtime. Otherwise, it was pretty good.'

Rick shrugged. 'Par for the course. So, about that drink? I know a cozy little place just off the high street, candles, jazz music, all that….'

'I thought a few of you were going?'

Rick shrugged. 'Well, I mentioned I might be going out to Old Don—'

'The guy in the tweed jacket and with the comb-over? I'm sure you'll have a lovely time.'

'Well, I doubt he'd actually show up—'

Jennifer lifted an eyebrow. 'So, who else have you asked?'

'So far, just you.' Rick lifted a suggestive eyebrow that

made him look like something out of a men's shampoo advert. 'I like to keep things … close.'

Behind Jennifer, Amy made a throwing up noise. She smiled. 'Well, I'm kind of busy tonight, but maybe, we'll see. How about you go and wait there, and maybe I'll come later. Sound good?'

Rick gave what Jennifer could only describe as a shunned pout. 'Don't be late,' he said. 'If I wear my Burberry, the seat opposite won't stay vacant for long.'

'Not if Don shows up.'

Amy sniggered. Rick looked about to retort, when Greg clapped his hands at the front of the room.

'Right, everyone, please sit down. Thanks for showing up and not crying off with some doctors' appointment or other rubbish. I wanted to talk about the harvest festival, due to be held on October 16th. You've all been preparing your classes for it, I assume?'

'Planted pumpkins back in May,' Rick muttered under his breath. 'Still waiting for the buggers to fruit.'

'Well, I'm afraid there's some bad news. Unless you like a challenge and a bit of adversity, in which case it's good news.'

'The postal service finally agreed to take you back?' grunted Don from near the front. 'Leaving our ship rudderless?'

Greg rolled his eyes, trying to ignore the sniggers. 'The school board has decided to resurface the playground this school year, and the only time the contractors are available is from mid-September through October. So unfortunately we can't use the playground. And the dining hall is out, because preparations would leave us without space for P.E. or assemblies for a couple of weeks. As a result, I've spoken to the council, and they've suggested we use the community centre on Porter Street.'

'It's a caravan!' Rick shouted. 'You couldn't fit one class in that.'

'It's a temporary structure, I'm aware,' Greg said. 'The old one was unfortunately torn down last year due to damp issues in the walls. However, I'm sure you're all resourceful enough to pull through.'

Amy sniffed into a handkerchief. 'My kids have worked so hard,' she said. 'They've made these lovely little posters, and they were going to do a dance—'

'We'll have to cancel any songs or performances,' Greg said. 'Unfortunately there won't be the space.'

Amy began to sob.

'Look at her,' Rick muttered, leaning close to Jennifer. 'What a crybaby.' He leaned across in front of Jennifer, making her flinch away from his aftershave. 'Look on the bright side, Clair. Less staying late, less working weekends—'

'I don't care!'

At the front, Greg clapped his hands together again. 'Right, well, that's about it. The meeting's over.'

Some teachers shuffled out to head back to their form rooms or to go home. Greg disappeared into his office, and Rick pulled his jacket off the back of his chair and swung it around his shoulders with a flourish.

'Right, ladies, I'll be on my way. Brentwell's finest will be lining the streets in expectation. See you later, Jenny. Enjoy your night in, Clair.'

Amy narrowed her eyes as Rick departed, then wiped her nose with a tissue and resumed her current task, which was emptying tiny paper circles out a box of pink hole punches.

'Wow, he really likes you,' she said to Jennifer. 'Good luck with that.'

'I suppose some people must find him attractive,'

Jennifer said with a smile. 'He has a certain teenage charm. Whenever he speaks I want to swat him like a fly.'

'You're not really going to meet him, are you?'

'I'd rather stay in and watch the news all night,' Jennifer said. 'He's not really my type, and anyway….'

'You have a boyfriend?'

Jennifer smiled, then let it drop. She didn't need to go there right now. 'I'd better get going,' she said. 'The dog and cat will be craving my attention. It really is bad news about the harvest festival, isn't it?'

Amy nodded, then quickly covered her mouth with the handkerchief before she could sob all over Jennifer's desk.

WHEN JENNIFER LEFT HALF an hour later, Rick was still hanging about in the staff car park, leaning against his car and playing on his phone as though waiting for someone. To avoid an unnecessary confrontation, she slipped back into the school before he had seen her and went out of the front entrance instead. This route would add a few minutes to her walk home, but according to an email Greg had sent out, Porter Street was only a couple of extra minutes north, so Jennifer decided to swing past and have a look at the new site of their harvest festival for herself.

At her last school, where the kids were decidedly more on the devilish side than those at Brentwell Primary, her only real memory of the harvest festival was of a couple of delinquent Year Sixes setting fire to the straw man the Year Ones had spent the entire month preparing. The wind had blown the flames on to the awning of a neighbouring fruit and vegetable stall, the fire brigade had been summoned, and the whole festival had been abandoned.

While she didn't expect such extreme circumstances to

be repeated, she hardly felt enthusiastic, and so far her struggle to survive her first week had left her with no energy even to think about it. On Greg's official programme her class was supposed to organise a cake stall, but what that entailed she was yet to work out.

She only had to consult her phone's map a couple of times to find Porter Street, but when she turned down the narrow cul-de-sac and found herself face to face with the community centre, she felt a sinking feeling inside. It wasn't quite the caravan Rick had claimed, but it was a cabin, probably large enough for about twenty people. In front was a weed-strewn, gravel parking area full of ruts and puddles. On one side was an abandoned car garage, its sign faded, paint peeling, while the other backed on to a recycling plant, a tall, rusty panel fence topped with barbed wire, stinging nettles growing in clumps around its base.

What joy the children would feel when they saw it. Jennifer was tempted to set the cabin on fire herself; at least that way they could get a little autumn colour. She went a little closer, wandering around the back of the cabin, where a cluster of broken bottles were choking in the weeds, and someone had spray-painted a large curse word in red paint on the recycling plant's fence.

She sighed. Perhaps it would be better if Greg cancelled the festival altogether.

6

HAUNTINGS

THE DIRECT ROUTE back to Jennifer's flat from Porter Street led down through the north entrance to Sycamore Park. The smells of fresh cooking greeted her as she approached the Oak Leaf Café. Outside, several tables were occupied, and through the open door Jennifer saw Angela bustling about in the kitchen, preparing orders.

There appeared to be no one else on duty, so Jennifer went inside, leaned over the counter and called Angela's name.

'Are you all right in there? Would you like some help?'

Angela turned around. When she recognised Jennifer, she gave a wide smile and clasped her hands in front of her heart.

'If you could save my life and help with the next couple of orders, you can eat for free for the next week,' she said. 'The lad I had on this afternoon called in sick, and I just got a big takeaway order for a family party.' She nodded at a line of hanging aprons by the door. 'Come in and put one of those on.'

It had been a long time since Jennifer had done

anything in a kitchen other than select a microwave setting, but Angela soon had her buzzing around, peeling and chopping, kneading, folding and basting, stirring, pouring and sprinkling. Within half an hour, they had fulfilled the current orders and had three pies baking in the oven ready for the Saturday rush.

'Fantastic,' Angela said, pulling off her apron and clapping flour off her hands with two hard sideways strokes. 'You're raw, but I could train you.'

'Thanks.'

'And I really appreciate it. I'm getting a little long in the tooth, so it's tough these days when we get busy. I suppose I could put away a couple of the tables, but you should never turn down business. One of the rules, isn't it?'

Jennifer nodded. 'I guess so.'

'Right, well, now we've got all the customers sorted, you sit yourself down and I'll see what I can find for you. I'm trusting you haven't eaten yet?'

Jennifer shook her head. 'I had to stay late for a meeting.'

Angela rolled her eyes. 'Typical schools. Did someone leave the taps on in the toilets or pull out all the hand towels?'

'Nothing so deathly serious. It was about the harvest festival. They can't hold it at the school, so they've selected this ghastly community centre on Porter Street instead.'

'Oh, I know it. The caravan?'

'It's not quite a caravan, but it's about the same size. And the car park is gravel so it'll be horrible for setting up any stalls. It's going to be a disaster.'

Angela grinned. 'I heard the old place was haunted, so they tore it down.'

'Seriously?'

Angela shrugged. 'It would make a better story than

blaming the demolition on damp. It was probably a spiteful imp that haunted the mains water pipes.'

'Well, they couldn't possibly have chosen a worse place. The kids will hate it.'

Angela frowned. 'Why don't you just hold it here in Sycamore Park?'

'Is that allowed?'

'I don't see why not. I'll have a word with Tom, the park's caretaker, when he comes in for breakfast. He always does on a Saturday morning. He'll know for sure.'

Jennifer thought for a moment, then nodded. 'Great, thanks.'

Angela smiled, then went back into the kitchen. From her usual window seat, Jennifer watched the park outside, where shadows were just beginning to lengthen beneath the trees as the sun dipped behind the theatre.

It was worth a try. Plus, if she could do something good for the school it would gain a few brownie points with Greg. Jennifer had survived her first week by the skin of her teeth, but still considered herself on probation. Many of the kids were still cold with her, and some of the older teachers turned their noses up as though aware of how she was stumbling through each day.

Angela reappeared with a plate of seasonal salad, a bowl of pumpkin soup, and a large slice of lamb and rosemary pie, all precariously balanced on her forearms. She set it down in front of Jennifer like an old pro, then produced a bottle of wine and two glasses.

'If you don't mind,' she said. 'I just called last orders, and it is Friday after all. You'll allow an old lady to indulge, won't you? I don't quite have the legs for the clubs on the high street, but I can handle a couple of glasses of wine before slippers and bed.'

'Just the one,' Jennifer said, taking her glass and

holding it out. 'Bonky needs his evening walk and James will be getting hungry. But it is Friday, so best make it a large.'

LATER, sitting on her sofa with her feet up on her coffee table, Bonky asleep on her lap and James nestled in beside her, Jennifer sipped a cup of hot chocolate and congratulated herself on surviving her first week. Last Monday, watching the removal men carrying boxes into the flat, still unsure where Brentwell Primary actually was in location to her new address, and unaware of the existence of a wonderful park just a five-minute walk away, Jennifer couldn't have imagined that by the end of her first school week, she would have made a new friend, learned how to cook a quiche, and become a lobbyist for the survival of an ancient tree.

Neither would she have expected to have to clean up three different piles of sick, rescue a plimsoll, break up a fight, and become a new object of desire for the local womaniser.

Brentwell was certainly throwing up the surprises.

Her phone rang, making her jerk out of a half-doze. James, annoyed, jumped down and made his way over to his basket on another chair. Bonky rolled over, then settled again.

Jennifer looked at the picture flashing up on her phone, an older, more matured version of herself. She steeled herself, then answered the call.

'Hi, Mum.'

'Ah, so you haven't lost it after all.'

Jennifer sighed. 'I just needed a little radio silence for a few days. Just until I'd got myself sorted out.'

'Even from your own mother? Honestly, what's the world coming to? Did you do what you needed to do? Can I call my only daughter again now?'

'Yeah, it's fine.'

'Just fine? I'd hoped it would be more than that. Do you know how worried I've been? I know you wanted your father and I to respect your decisions and everything, but you're still my daughter. I still have the right to know what's going on.'

Jennifer said nothing. There was a question she had hoped to avoid as long as possible, but she had known it would come eventually. She took a deep breath.

'Mark … how is he?'

'Oh, so you do still care, after running out on him.'

'I didn't—'

'What else would you call it?'

'I—'

'He's fine, for what it's worth. He wanted to know where you were, but your father and I respected your wishes. Well, that silly note you put under our door. I thought it was a joke at first, but your father told me your handwriting hadn't changed much since you used to write him those little letters as a kid. In fact, I would have spoken to Mark if it hadn't been for him talking me around.'

Jennifer smiled. Her Mum was obsessed with appearances and doing the perceived "right thing", but her dad had always had her back.

'I don't want Mark to know where I am. He'll just show up, make a scene, start trying to convince me that I'm wrong, that everything was fine … when it wasn't.'

On the other end of the line, her mother sighed. 'You had everything. I don't know what you're playing at throwing it away.'

Jennifer tried to answer, but none of the words on her

tongue made any sense. After a few seconds of silence, she shook her head. 'It's late,' she said. 'I need to go to bed.'

'Jennifer—'

Too late, Jennifer hung up. Before her mother could call her again, she switched off her phone and tossed it away to the other end of the sofa, out of reach. Bonky grumbled and rolled over again. With her fingers gently massaging his back, Jennifer stared at the wall, wondering, for the millionth time, whether she had done the right thing.

7

SECRET PLANS

BONKY WOKE her up just before sunrise. With a groan, Jennifer leaned over and pulled the energetic little dog up onto her bed. James, sleeping on the duvet near her feet, yawned and jumped down as the dog's excitement threatened to overspill, resuming sentry duty on the windowsill, through which a grey light was filtering in.

Wishing for a couple of hours of extra sleep but unable to refuse the dog's requests, particularly as she still felt guilty for getting home late yesterday, Jennifer got up, fed her fur-children and then made coffee. The dawn sunlight was just filtering in through her kitchen window when she collected Bonky's lead and headed out.

The air was crisp, the wind chilly when it gusted. Bonky didn't seem to care as he inspected the lamp posts on the way to Sycamore Park, but Jennifer kept her hands deep in her jacket pockets, the dog's lead wrapped around one wrist.

Sycamore Park looked wonderful just after sunrise, with the sunlight glinting off the first leaves to change colour. Crows and pigeons called from the branches, and from the direction of the pond came the frantic quacking of ducks. Jennifer nodded hello to a handful of other dog walkers, some of whom she already recognised from previous visits. Most were older people, but a couple were younger women like herself, and with each shared smile she felt the pull of potential friendship.

Near the southern entrance, a portable burger van was just setting up, several people already waiting in line, blowing on their hands to ward off the cold. Jennifer did a loop of the park, past the closed Oak Leaf Café and through the courtyard around Big Gerry, and was heading back in the direction of the burger van when she saw a short, plump figure in unflattering jogging bottoms huffing and puffing along the path towards her.

It was unlikely the girl wanted to be seen, but short of making a run for Big Gerry's expansive trunk, Jennifer had no way to hide herself. As Amy Clairmont approached, Jennifer lifted a tentative hand in greeting.

Amy looked up, gave an exhausted gasp, and shuddered to a halt like a broken down train.

'Oh. Oh my.'

'Good morning. I'm, ah, just walking my dog. Do you come jogging here every day?'

Amy, her cheeks a violent red, a headband pushing her hair up into a mushroom cloud, pushed foggy spectacles up her nose. 'Oh, no, it's just … a new term and all … that.'

'I'm sorry to disturb you. I live just round the corner. I'll let you get on.'

It was clear that Amy, now stopped, would never get started again. She leaned on her knees, drawing in great, gasping breaths.

'It's okay … I'm about done.'

Jennifer smiled. 'Well, in that case, do you want to grab a coffee from that van? It's a bit chilly this morning.'

Amy looked up, stared at Jennifer for a few seconds as though grasping for the energy to speak, then nodded. 'Ah … sure. Plus a bottle of water.'

They headed over to the burger van, where the line had got a little longer, people queuing for coffee, tea, and hot breakfast rolls. When their turn came, the proprietor, a middle-aged man with a glistening bald head and a kind smile nodded at Amy.

'Hello again, Amy. Been a while. The usual? Double pork roll?'

Amy, clearly friends with the man, nodded. 'Thanks, Pete. Extra mayonnaise, but hold the chilli sauce.'

'I'll put in a leaf of lettuce just for balance,' Pete said, giving her a wink. 'Who's your friend?'

'Jennifer,' Jennifer said. 'I live round the corner. Just moved in this week.'

'Well, lovely to meet you. The name's Pete, Pete Markham. You'll find me here every Saturday and Sunday, sun, rain, wind or snow, if we were ever lucky enough to get any. And if you ever get married, I'm your man.'

Amy gave a little titter, and Jennifer wondered if she'd missed some joke.

'Okay, sure.'

Pete rolled his eyes at Amy, then gave an apologetic smile to Jennifer. 'I meant for catering. This is a side gig. I can go full gourmet if you need. Website's down there.' He leaned forward and pointed at the side of the van underneath the serving window.

'Thanks.'

'So welcome to Sycamore Park. I hope to see you around.'

'Pete does the best pulled pork roll in Brentwell,' Amy said, sweat dripping off her face as she smiled.

'Ah, but if you want proper food, go and see Angela up at the Oak Leaf over there,' Pete said.

Jennifer smiled. 'We've met,' she said. 'And you're right, the food is great.'

'The best,' Pete said. 'But since she's not open yet, what can I get you? Another double pork?'

Jennifer would have preferred something a little healthier, but Amy had a conspiratorial look in her eyes, and it was Saturday after all.

'Go on, then,' she said. 'And the largest coffee that you do.'

'Coming right up.'

THEY TOOK their coffees and pork rolls to a bench near the duck pond that was warmed by the morning sun through the trees. Jennifer let Bonky off his lead to wander among the bushes by the waterside, then held her disposable coffee cup in both hands to warm them. Amy, buoyed by her morning run, gulped down a bottle of water and then chewed through her roll almost as quickly. She wiped her mouth on her sleeve, suppressed a belch, then turned to Jennifer.

'So, how was your first week? You're still here, so it must have gone okay.'

'Up and down,' Jennifer said. 'I can only remember about half my kids' names, and twice this week I took them to the music room instead of to the gym, but otherwise, I'm surviving.'

'No melted jelly beans on your seat yet?'

'Ah, no.'

Amy gave a sage nod. 'Keep an eye on Danny Long. His brother Rick is in my class, and I'm sure he was the instigator. How they'd know I'd be wearing white trousers on Wednesday, I have no idea. The worst thing is that I didn't even notice until lunchtime, so it had dried hard.'

'I'll check my chairs,' Jennifer said.

Amy gave a snorted laugh. 'It still tasted okay, though. A bit woody from the benches in the playground, but not too bad.' Then, with a cough and a smile, she added, 'I'm just joking. I dropped it in Christopher's coffee.'

'Who?'

Amy slapped the bench and laughed. 'Oh, that's another, sorry. A bit in-depth, that one. Christopher Priest, he's a science fiction writer. Priest, get it? *The Inverted World*? Great book. Clara was obsessed.'

'Mrs. Goldsmith?'

'Yeah, loved her sci-fi. Asimov, Frank Herbert, Larry Niven, John Daulton, always had a book in her hands. We had a competition last Christmas for who could come up with the best one. Obviously only select staff were involved. Maud, for example, would have grassed.'

'Sounds fun.'

'Yeah, it was.' Amy sighed. 'Ah … Clara, she was a shining light.'

'Oh. That's great.'

Amy looked up suddenly. 'I didn't mean it like that. You're just as nice. And you know, everyone has to retire sometime.'

'Yeah.'

As though the mood had been severed with a poisoned sword, Amy looked at her watch. 'Well, I'd better get going. Got my script to work on before Monday. You'll be there after school, won't you?'

'Um, where?'

'At rehearsals.'

'What rehearsals?'

'For the teachers' play. We do one for the harvest festival every year. It'll be a bit of a dampener, of course, because Porter Street's community centre doesn't really have the space, but we'll still have fun.'

Jennifer's head was reeling from too much information. 'Um, didn't Greg say there were to be no class dramas?'

'This isn't a class drama. This is the teachers' drama.'

'Isn't that a little unfair?'

Amy sniffed. A tear dropped out of her eye and dribbled down her cheek to mingle with the beads of sweat still hanging precariously to her chin.

'But Clara worked so hard. It was her parting gift to us. We have to perform it, even if it's in … secret.'

'Right,' Jennifer said, feeling yet another slap of inadequacy strike her across the cheek like a hard lump of solidified autumn wind.

'So you'll be there?'

Jennifer gave a grim nod. 'I'll be there.'

8

NEW ACQUAINTANCES

A LITTLE RETAIL therapy felt in order, so after unpacking some more boxes, Jennifer headed into town, wandering up and down Brentwell's high street, browsing a surprisingly varied selection of specialist shops, picking up a few things for her kitchen, even buying a set of curtains for the bedroom to give James something to hide behind while he kept watch. She was only spotted by three kids from her class out shopping with their parents: Kelly and Becky Jarder, who squealed with excitement when they spotted her in Primark, hiding behind their mother who gave Jennifer an embarrassed smile, then Matthew Bridges and his mother in the greengrocer. Matthew gave her a polite hello, before bending to pick up a couple of apples his mother had dropped on the floor. The woman, frail and thin-faced, smiled at Jennifer and nodded, before heading out, leaning on a stick with one hand, Matthew helping her with the other, the bag of apples bouncing over his shoulder. Jennifer watched them go with a sense of aching in her heart.

She bought a sandwich for lunch in a bakery then sat

outside in the town square to watch the world go by. As always when she allowed herself too much time to think, the doubts about her decision to move started to creep in, but Brentwell was a pretty little town, even if its size meant that due to her status as a teacher at the local primary she would soon become familiar wherever she went.

At least she was back in control. She had her own place, her own job. No one telling her where to go, what to do, when to get up, what to wear, when and how to spend her money.

She closed her eyes for a moment, feeling like an impulsive sod for the mess she had knowingly left behind. It would catch up with her eventually, but for now it was best to put it out of her mind and focus on the future she had chosen.

A future on her own.

WHEN SHE CAME out of a bookshop a little after three o'clock, clouds had rolled in and rain was darkening the streets. Having not brought either an umbrella or a jacket, Jennifer hurried for the sanctuary of a little town museum at the end of the street. Inside, she browsed displays of old farming equipment, pictures of the restoration of the church, relics from an old canal now choked in weeds and mostly buried. Jennifer bought a couple of pretty coasters from a woman who looked vaguely familiar. As the woman put her coasters into a paper bag, Jennifer noticed the name tag on her staff uniform.

Marlie Gordon.

It was a common surname, but Jennifer, who hadn't really spoken to anyone since Amy in the park earlier, couldn't resist.

'Excuse me, you wouldn't happen to be Gavin Gordon's mother, by any chance?'

Marlie's eyes widened. She was pretty in a drawn kind of way, perhaps only a year or two older than Jennifer, but had dark circles around her eyes to suggest sleep was a bonus, rather than a privilege.

'Yes, that's right.'

'I'm his new teacher at Brentwell Primary.' Jennifer stuck out a hand and introduced herself. Marlie had a warm but calloused palm as though this wasn't her only job. 'I saw your name and took a guess. It's not that big a town, is it?'

Marlie smiled. 'No, you get to know pretty much everyone.' She looked down, giving an apologetic smile to the desktop. 'I'm sorry if Gavin's a little … disruptive. His father and I … we separated last year, and Gavin doesn't really see much of him now. He was always a lively lad, but he's never been … bad.'

'Well, I don't think—'

Marlie looked up and gave a little shake of the head. 'You don't need to make excuses to me. I know how he is.'

'He has a lot of energy. I wish he'd channel it into his schoolwork.'

Marlie laughed, a light, despondent titter. 'Or into helping me. I'm not sure what to do.'

Jennifer was about to suggest that they go for a coffee to discuss it, but another staff member called to Marlie that a delivery van had just arrived.

'That's the new postcards,' Marlie said with a smile. 'I'd better go and sort them out. It was nice to meet you, Jennifer. I hope you'll be a good influence on my son.' She sighed. 'I'm not doing such a great job myself.'

They parted ways, Marlie heading off to sort the new postcards, Jennifer back out into the town, where the rain had thankfully stopped. She walked up the high street, waved to a couple of tittering pupils hiding behind their parents' legs, then headed for home.

As she walked down the street towards the north entrance to Sycamore Park, she found Angela outside the Oak Leaf Café, clearing tables.

'Oh, hi there,' she said. 'Thanks again for yesterday.'

'No problem. Any time.'

'Were you busy today?'

Angela pouted. 'The rain was a pain, as they say. There are only so many I can fit inside, but those pies will still be good tomorrow. I usually close Monday and Tuesday, so I'll make another batch Tuesday night.'

Jennifer had a brief pang of longing that her new friend would be unavailable at the beginning of the week, but there was always her flat's new cooker that could be christened with a dish or two. Other than using it to boil water before she unpacked the kettle, she was yet to cook anything at home.

'Oh, by the way, Tom's in today, so if you like, I could ask him to come over and we could chat about your harvest festival.'

'Tom?'

'The park's caretaker?'

'Oh.' Jennifer paused a moment, unsure whether she had the energy to talk to some old gardener about yet another school issue. It seemed that everywhere she went, she was faced with more school issues. And while it was nice to take her mind off what she had left behind, she felt like she wasn't really getting a break.

Angela lifted an eyebrow. 'Too much shopping?' She smiled. 'I'll make you a coffee while we wait. Go and sit down. I'll give him a bell.'

Jennifer went inside and sat at her usual window table

while Angela pulled an old Nokia out of her pocket. Jennifer watched her through the windows as she walked among the tables, her voice inaudible but the tone of the conversation obvious from the way she laughed, smiled, and gestured as she spoke. Jennifer wondered where the woman got her energy. If there was a secret elixir pond somewhere in Sycamore Park, she would like to see it.

Angela came back inside, rubbing her bare arms. 'Gosh, it's getting chilly. That means the leaves will start to fall soon. Once they start to pile up, be careful where Bonky puts his nose.'

'Snakes?'

Angela laughed. 'No, hedgehogs. Prickly little things. I have a hibernation box round the back. Last year we had babies.'

'Sounds … interesting.'

'The local kids were dead excited. We might end up with more this spring, although there are none in the box yet. Oh, Tom said he'll be over in a bit. I'll just get those coffees.'

Jennifer yawned. It seemed like a long time ago that Bonky was barking her out of bed.

Angela returned with two cups heaped with cream and brown marshmallows. Jennifer stared as Angela put the sugary monstrosity down in front of her.

'Seasonal mocha blend,' Angela explained. 'You looked a little sleepy, so I figured a sugar hit would help. And of course, some marshmallows. They're homemade. I get them online from a cottage shop in the Lake District.'

'They're … brown.'

'Chestnut flavour. Seasonal, I told you. Although I imagine they're last year's chestnuts, as ours won't start falling for another month.'

Jennifer couldn't help but laugh. 'It looks fantastic.'

'I've got some walnut biscuits if you want one.'

'I'll be fine, but thanks.'

Grinning, Angela looked about to offer something else when the bell over the front door tinkled.

'Ah, here's Tom.'

The door opened and the park caretaker entered. Jennifer stared. Instead of the old, bent, perhaps grey-bearded geriatric with hands gnarled like old tree roots that she had expected, Tom was around thirty-five, well over six feet tall, and wide enough at the shoulders that he looked capable of pulling trees out of the ground. Both his eyes and the hair that stuck up in wind-ruffled tufts were the colour of hazelnut, and he wore an easy, kind smile.

'Sorry to keep you waiting,' he said.

'Quite all right.' Angela gestured to a chair. 'Have a seat. I'll just get your coffee.'

She got up and went back into the kitchen, leaving Jennifer and Tom alone. The park caretaker sat down, and stuck out a big, bearlike hand.

'Tom,' he said. 'You must be Jennifer? It's nice to meet you.'

Jennifer just stared. Finally, by the time Tom had started to chuckle, she was able to find enough breath to mutter, 'Uh.'

9

CHASING DUCKS

J ENNIFER WOKE up on Sunday feeling like an idiot. So fan-girl dumbstruck by Tom's appearance, she had needed Angela to relay most of the details in a coherent manner. And Tom, seemingly oblivious to Jennifer's idolatry, had simply shrugged and said he would check with the council. After fifteen minutes, during which Jennifer had spoken perhaps ten words, Tom bade them farewell and left.

Angela, with a knowing look on her face, had said little, exchanging a few vague pleasantries before packing Jennifer off home with a bag containing half a walnut pie and a pot of beef and pumpkin stew.

Bonky needed his morning walk, but Jennifer was in the mood to get away from Brentwell for a while. She put the dog in the car and drove out into the country, to a pretty little village called Willow River, where she walked along a cycle path for a while before getting lunch at a pleasant country pub called the Harvest Inn. The air was cool, the wind rustling through the tree branches, the leaves beginning to change colour. She ate lunch at a picnic table in the beer garden which overlooked a pretty river, willow branches trailing in the water.

On the way back, she drove past fields of browned corn, others with hay bales already dotted across their swathes of cut grass. Only a few weeks and winter would be in full swing, bringing with it the storms and rain that made British winter so unpleasant. Despite the chill, she wound down her window to let the wind tickle her face and the smell of freshly cut grass drift in.

Autumn was the best season, she thought. Fine weather, beautiful colours, but also a season of change, of fresh starts.

She drove back home, enjoying a glass of wine with her dinner—what was left of Angela's pumpkin stew and a couple of cakes she had picked up from a local shop not far from the Harvest Inn.

Her first week in Brentwell—the first week of a new life —was almost over. It had been interesting, to say the least.

HER SECOND WEEK in Brentwell was a slightly diluted version of the first. Rick hit on her just a little less, Amy's eccentricities felt just a little less strange, and her class felt just a little less threatening. She found out another of Greg's nicknames was Foggy; not however after the famous *Last of the Summer Wine* character, but after Father John Misty, the American singer, and a favourite of a particularly hip teacher who had left a couple of years ago to become a parachuting instructor.

'Rick *hated* him,' Amy said, as she sliced the tops off a series of glue sticks with a paper cutter, then lined them all up to make sure they were even. 'Too many big dogs in the yard and all that.'

'I can imagine,' Jennifer said.

Matthew Bridges was unexpectedly absent for a couple of days during midweek, prompting Jennifer to make a call to his parents. His father answered, and told Jennifer in an apologetic voice that Matthew's mother had gone into hospital for another operation, and that the boy didn't feel up to school at the moment. Jennifer offered to bring around some homework at the weekend.

After school on Friday was the first read-through for the teachers' drama. Jennifer hadn't heard anything back from Angela about the possibility of staging the harvest festival in Sycamore Park, so said nothing to the other teachers, just in case they were stuck with the potentially haunted cabin on Porter Street after all. As the teachers, most of them grumbling about having to stay late, filed into the staffroom after the last school buses had left, Amy walked among the desks, handing out copies of a script.

Rick, one hand on the back of Jennifer's chair, one leg cocked behind the other, chuckled as he took his script from Amy and said, 'So, of course I'm the lead?'

'It's an ensemble cast,' Amy said.

'And what does that mean? So we get to pick our parts?'

Amy sighed. 'It means that no one part is greater than the other. Several parts could be considered the lead.'

'But I'm more lead than the others?'

'Just read it,' Jennifer said, as Amy shrugged.

'Look who's itching for the pub,' Rick said, giving Jennifer a grin. Then, calling out to Amy, he said, 'Single life is tough, eh, Clair? Never knowing if your last boyfriend will prove your, well, last.' He grinned again. 'Or your first.'

Amy pouted and looked about to burst into tears. 'Leave her alone,' Jennifer said.

'I'm just having a joke, eh, Clair? You and me, we're buddies really, aren't we?'

Amy just scowled and scurried mouse-like away, handing out scripts to a couple of older teachers who took them with frustrated sighs.

'I only have one line,' moaned Mrs. Tellings, the part-time specialist home economics teacher. '"Is it bread you want, or eggs?" What the hell is that supposed to mean? Are you taking the—'

'I didn't write it,' Amy said, cheeks red.

'You can have a few of mine,' said Old Don Jones, the Year Six teacher. 'You're wanting me to memorise all this, Amy? I can barely remember the kid's names.'

'It'll help stave off dementia,' Rick muttered under his breath, leaning close enough to Jennifer that she waved a hand to swat him away.

'I didn't write it,' Amy said again, a little tremble in her voice that made Jennifer want to go and hold her hand.

The door opened and Greg walked in. An immediate hush fell over the room. Greg, who wasn't part of the production, glanced at a script sitting on the nearest desk and gave a little chuckle.

'Easy life, you lot have. Back when I started out we were expected to actually work.'

'What happened to your meeting?' Don said. 'You lose your map, or did your tag go off?'

Greg glared at him as others chuckled. 'It got moved to Tuesday. I'll be off home now. You lot remember to turn the kettles and the lights off at five. The council have been on our backs about the budget these last couple of weeks. I'd hate to have to cancel the harvest festival altogether.'

He picked up his bag, and with another chuckle, headed out. As he left, Jennifer turned to Rick.

'What was that about his tag?'

Rick laughed. 'The old man got done for stalking his ex-wife last year. She got a restraining order taken out.'

'And he has a tag?'

Rick winced. 'Well, unless you want to get close enough to the old lion to pull up his trouser leg and check, we'll just have to assume. He reckons it was all a misunderstanding.'

Jennifer shook her head. 'Isn't there anyone normal around here?'

'Me!' Amy said, sticking a hand up in the air like an eager pupil. 'I'm normal.'

BONKY WAS SCRATCHING at the door when Jennifer got home, far later than she had intended. After one bad-tempered read through of the script, the teachers had voted to continue in the local pub across the street. Things had got worse rather than better, with Don Jones—playing a knight—squaring off against Colin Triller, the caretaker, who was playing a dragon. As their mock joust got a little exaggerated, Colin accidentally knocked over Don's pint, at which point Don offered to thump him for real, his comb-over flapping up and down like an excited butterfly. By the time things had calmed down, apologies had grudgingly been offered and pints refilled, it was getting late. Jennifer pretended to go to the toilet and then slipped out without saying goodbye.

Something that was becoming a bit of a habit, she thought with regret, as she led Bonky along Willis Lane to Sycamore Park. Her mother had tried to call a couple more times during the week, but Jennifer had refused to answer, instead sending a message to say she was busy. It hadn't been a strict lie—she had been working hard to keep up with school, as well as sort out her flat. It was finally beginning to look like a home, even though she still had a couple of boxes to unpack. She would get to those tomorrow, but part of her was dreading it all being done, because then she would have time left to think, and when she had time to think, she began to doubt everything.

Even though she had walked out of Mark's life without warning, vowing never to return, when she looked at it objectively, she wondered if she had made a big mistake. He hadn't done anything to hurt her; he hadn't been abusive or unkind. The old cliché kept popping up like a laughing jack-in-the-box: *it's not you, it's me.*

It was partly true at least.

The air was chilly tonight, and the first leaves were starting to fall from the trees. Even though the air left the tip of Jennifer's nose feeling a little numb, Sycamore Park had a majestic autumn beauty, all browns and oranges, showers of falling leaves cascading across the path every time the wind blew. Through the buildings to the west the evening sun glittered off the ripples on the duck pond, and Jennifer led Bonky along the path to where the birds were waddling about. He looked keen to chase a few, but just as Jennifer leaned down to unclip his lead, she caught sight of a figure through the bushes, crouching low.

She felt a momentary panic that this was some stalker or weirdo, perhaps even Mark having finally tracked her down. Her breath caught in her throat before the figure moved, and to her relief she saw he was facing the other way, crouched down on the grass, some kind of metal pole in his hands. As she watched, frowning, he shuffled forward, then made a sudden jerk, before falling flat on his face.

As the man let out an exasperated grunt, Jennifer stood up to see better. It was Tom, the park caretaker, with a fisherman's net in his hands. In wellington boots and a forest green parka jacket, he appeared to be stalking one of the ducks.

She frowned again. The one time she had met him last week, his looks had overwhelmed her somewhat, even though the kind of guy who worked as a park caretaker had to be a little rough around the edges. Surely it was illegal to catch wild ducks for food, but that looked to be exactly what he was doing.

It was still daylight and there were a few joggers and dog walkers around. Feeling emboldened, Jennifer stood up and walked up behind him, Bonky panting on his lead. Wishing she had brought her phone so she could film Tom in the act, Jennifer cleared her throat, and said, 'Excuse me. I don't think you should be doing that.'

Tom, surprised, jerked forward and fell flat on his face again. As he scrambled around, his look of shock changed to one of amusement. He brushed himself down and stood up, giving Jennifer a warm smile.

'Do you think you could do me a favour?' he asked. 'I'm going to be here all night at this rate, and if I don't get him, a cat will.'

'Who?'

'Him over there. Francis.'

'Francis?'

'Francis Drake. The proud little chap over there. He's got a broken wing, so he's not going to do well with the girls this autumn until I can get him to a vet.'

Jennifer frowned, before understanding what he meant. The male duck was waddling along the side of the pond, one wing slightly protruding from his back, a little bent and out of place. When Tom crept closer, other ducks took to flight or to the water, but Francis carried on waddling along the water side, quacking with irritated regularity.

'If you could tie your dog to the tree there, and creep around the other side, that would be great. I've been after him for ages but he keeps giving me the slip.'

Jennifer, wondering if she was getting into some weird kind of comedy routine, did as Tom asked. Squatting low and spreading her arms, she tried to direct the duck back into the path of Tom's net.

'Watch out, it's a bit wet over there,' Tom said, then suddenly winced as Jennifer found out for herself, stepping into a patch of mud and sinking nearly up to her ankle. She stared down at her vanished foot in horror, only the outline of a trainer in the brown slime proving her foot hadn't been chopped right off.

'Oops, too late. I've got a towel in the shed over there,' so don't worry.'

Jennifer grimaced. 'Uh, thanks. Do you happen to have a spare shoe?'

Tom shrugged. 'Might be a couple I've found lying around the place. You'd be surprised what people leave behind. Ah … gotcha!'

He gave a hoot of delight as the net came down over Francis's struggling body. Tom closed in like a professional hunter, calming the bird and tucking the trapped animal up under his arm.

'Let me just get him in a cage,' he said. 'Then we'll sort you out.'

'I think I'm sinking.'

'It goes down a long way over there. Three or four feet.'

At Jennifer's look of horror, Tom laughed. 'Joking. You're all good. Come on, lean on my shoulder. I'll get you out of there.'

With Francis under one arm, Tom held out the other for Jennifer to balance while she tried to pull her foot free.

She had to twist it around a little, the mud refusing to give it up, then with a sudden squelchy pop, her foot slipped out of the shoe, leaving the sock behind.

'Ah....'

'Hold Francis a moment.'

Jennifer took the wet, wriggling duck—still in the net—while Tom pulled her shoe and sock out of the mud, holding it up. 'It'll probably wash off, but it looks pretty cheap so you might be better off just buying a new pair.'

'Cheap! It wasn't—'

Tom shrugged. 'Just a suggestion.'

The shoes had cost fifteen pounds in Shoe Fayre, but Jennifer wasn't about to admit it. She took the soaking thing off Tom and passed him the duck, whose feet had left muddy stains on the front of her sweater.

'Thanks for the help,' Tom said, then gave Jennifer a smile which made the inklings of anger she had been feeling blink out. 'All in a day's work, eh?'

10

SEEKING HELP

Tom's maintenance shed, which was tucked among trees just south of the theatre on the west side of the park, seemed surprisingly large, and rather more homely than Jennifer had expected. One half was filled with tools and other equipment, but the front half had a couple of sofas around a small TV, a toilet, and a sink with running water.

While Jennifer washed her foot and rinsed her sock and trainer as best she could, Tom made tea and pulled a tin of biscuits out of a ramshackle, leaning cupboard. Francis had been transferred to a pet carry case, and Bonky, now that the bird was unavailable for chasing, had taken up residence on one of the old, slumped sofas.

'I'll get him off to the vet in the morning,' Tom said. 'He's been wandering around like that for a couple of days. Probably had a run in with a cat, or maybe even a kid on a bike. There are a few that come through the park that don't have much respect.'

'Will he be able to fly again?'

Tom smiled. 'Don't worry, I have a mate who's a vet. He'll sort him out. Francis will probably have to be kept locked up for a couple of weeks until his wing heals, but he'll be out chasing the girls again soon. It depends how serious it is, but I've seen a few like that, and it's probably an easy fix.'

'Do you name all the ducks?' Jennifer said, squeezing out her sock and hanging it on a dryer in front of a heater, alongside her shoe.

Tom winked. 'Of course.'

'I went to school with a girl called Francis Drake,' Jennifer said. 'She was a couple of years below me but I saw her around. I think Francis was her middle name, but some of the boys used to bully her about it.'

'Boys will be boys. There was a shop in my home town called Reynolds DIY, so for a while at school I was "Market Garden", for some random reason.' He grinned again. 'Until I grew big enough that no one would dare say it to my face anymore.'

Jennifer remembered the feel of Tom's shoulder muscles through his sweater when she had leaned on him, and gave a shy smile.

'I can imagine,' she said.

'Sorry again about not warning you about that wet patch. After the rain the other day, the pond level's a bit up from usual.'

'It's okay. It was … fun to help.'

'So what brought you to Brentwell? I heard from Angela that you've only been here a couple of weeks, and that you're working in the local primary.'

Jennifer wondered how much Angela might have said, although she'd not told her new friend any of the details. She wanted to keep it to herself, but Tom had a disarming look about him which made her feel like she could trust him. She sighed and shook her head.

'It's kind of complicated.'

'Oh.'

She wanted to tell him about Mark, but at the same time she was worried about what he might think. After all, even her mother failed to understand Jennifer's point of view. In the end, all she said was, 'I needed a change of scenery. Life was getting kind of … smothering.'

Tom gave a thoughtful nod. 'It can feel like that sometimes.' He spread his arms and smiled. 'Even for me.'

'And all you do is rake up leaves,' Jennifer said. She meant it as a joke, but from the change in Tom's eyes she suspected it had been taken the wrong way. 'I'm sorry, I didn't mean—'

'And catch ducks,' Tom said. 'Don't forget that.'

Jennifer patted her knees and stood up. 'I'd better get back,' she said. 'It's a long way in wet shoes.'

'Are you sure? If you wait half an hour—'

Jennifer shook her head, suddenly needing to leave. 'No, it's okay.'

'I can lend you some boots—'

'I have to get back. It's getting late.'

'Do you want me to walk you to the end of the park? It's getting dark out there now.'

'I'm fine.'

She had said it a little harsher than she had intended, but it was too late to go back on it now. Tom just looked hurt as she scooped her shoe and sock from the drying rack, stuffing the sock into her pocket and pulling the wet shoe over her bare foot. Then, grabbing Bonky's lead from where it hung over a chair, she picked up the little dog and staggered for the door, wincing as her cold, damp insole tickled her foot.

'It was nice to talk to you,' she said, trying to force a smile as she opened the door and felt the evening cold wrap around her. 'See you around?'

Tom said nothing but gave a brief shrug that could have meant anything. Jennifer, feeling equal parts relief and regret, slipped out, shutting the door behind her and hurrying off before she could either change her mind or Tom could come after her.

The sun had gone down and the park was shrouded in shadow. Flutters of falling leaves danced across the paths as she hurried for the way out. By the time she reached her flat, street lights had blinked on, and the air was decidedly cool. Inside, she switched on the heating, fed James and Bonky, then took a shower, washing her shoe and sock at the same time. She left them to dry by a radiator, then put on her pyjamas and took a bottle of wine from the fridge.

She thought about watching TV, but she wasn't in the mood. In the end, she sat on the sofa, drinking a glass of wine while staring at the wall, wondering what had happened to her. She liked Tom, she really did, but she couldn't go there right now. It had barely been two months since she had packed up her possessions and moved out of the house she had shared with Mark while he was away on yet another golfing weekend, leaving him the briefest of notes that it was over and she wouldn't be back. She felt like she had held up a pair of scissors to the storybook of her old life, but they had only cut part of the way through.

She could still remember Mark's number by heart. She could call him right now, and be back at her old place by tomorrow afternoon. Her old school would probably take her back, and all her old friends would forgive her.

Except they hadn't been her friends.

They had been Mark's.

And that had been part of the problem.

'I'm spoiled goods, Bonkster,' she said, patting the little dog sitting on her lap, while beside her, nestled against her thigh, James responded to her stroke with a deep, contented purr. 'I'm glad you guys are stupid enough to put up with me.'

SHE WOKE up the next morning feeling much the same as she had the night before, but with a hangover thrown into the mix. She made some cereal and took Bonky out for his walk, this time purposefully walking away from Sycamore Park along a series of bland suburban roads.

She realised it was time she got her feelings off her chest about Mark. A problem shared was a problem halved and all that. Making a roundabout route to Sycamore Park to avoid bumping into Tom, she knocked on Angela's back door, but got no answer. Around the front of the café the door had a sign: SORRY, OUT OF TOWN FOR THE DAY.

Frustrated, Jennifer sat down on a bench and thumbed through her phone's contact list. It was a pretty poor selection: unsympathetic family member, Mark-loyal friend, credit card replacement hotline, Mark-loyal friend, car mechanic, mother, Dottingham Animal clinic … she was about to give up, when she decided to check her recent calls.

Amy.

They must have exchanged numbers at the pub on Friday afternoon, and Jennifer hadn't gotten around to saving it to her contacts list. Amy wasn't exactly the first person she would choose to unload her darkest secrets upon, but she was a marginally better choice than Bonky or James, neither of whom were capable of offering much advice.

She made the call. Amy sounded surprised to get a

lunch invite, but quickly turned on the enthusiasm when Jennifer gave her the choice of location.

'See you in a couple of hours,' Jennifer said, hanging up.

～

THE RAJ of Punjab was a curry buffet restaurant in the centre of town. While not Jennifer's first choice, she didn't mind a bit of curry and it would probably help lift the hangover. Amy, waiting outside, was practically licking her lips with excitement as Jennifer waved and crossed the street.

'I've got us a table already,' Amy said, rubbing her hands together. 'Are you cold? I'm cold. Don't worry, we'll soon warm up in there. Do you know they have four types of Bhuna?'

'Are there four types?' Jennifer asked.

Amy grinned. 'Lamb, chicken, pork, and mixed meat,' she said.

'Oh.'

'Come on then, let's get started. I saw a family of big people go in just before. We have to hurry or they'll clean out all the onion bhajis.'

'Big people?'

Amy gave a nervous laugh, then puffed out her cheeks and flicked her eyes from side to side. Jennifer, fast regretting her decision to invite Amy for lunch, could at least see why she made a good teacher. The kids had to be endlessly entertained.

The table Amy had chosen was not just near the selection of curries, but right next to it, so that every time another customer got up to fill their plate, they would invariably spend some time leaning over Jennifer and

Amy's table while they reloaded their plates with thick Madras and korma sauces.

The food, however, Jennifer had to admit was pretty good, and within a few mouthfuls of hot, tasty curry, she was starting to feel a bit better. As a waiter brought over a heaped plate of sliced naan and poppadoms, she cleared her throat, wiped her mouth, and said, 'I hope you didn't mind me taking up your Saturday.'

Amy, resembling a hamster with her cheeks crammed full of thick chunks of chicken tikka, gave a frantic shake of her head. 'Oh, no, it's quite all right. A girls' day out and all that.'

'You must have been busy.'

Amy chuckled. 'Oh, you know, I had to clear a few things from my busy schedule, but you'll do that for a mate, won't you?'

'Thank you. I just needed some company. The dog and the cat … they're nice, but I like to talk to someone who can answer back from time to time.'

'No worries. You said on the phone you had something you wanted—oh, wait a moment. They just refilled the phaal. Blow your head off, that stuff will. Don't worry, you can have a bite of mine if you're scared.'

'I'm—' Jennifer began, but Amy was already out of her seat, flying low like a reconnaissance plane to slip between two enormous hill-sized people homing in on the most recently refilled curry vats. Jennifer watched with amusement as Amy squeezed in front of them to load her plate with phaal while one of them flapped a frustrated hand in protest, as though to swat away a fly.

'Look, it's okay,' Amy said, as she came and sat back down. 'I'm fine with it. I mean, I'm not one hundred percent fine, but I can live with it, if it's what you want.'

Jennifer frowned. 'If what's what I want?'

Amy stuffed a lump of pork into her mouth then leaned forward. 'Rick,' she said in a muffled voice. 'If you want to make a move on him, I'm cool. That's what this is about, isn't it?'

Jennifer winced. 'The only move I'd like to make on Rick is further away. At least a couple of desks, preferably another room entirely.'

Amy frowned. 'You mean … you're not … you're not interested in him?'

Jennifer laughed. 'Oh, I'm interested in him, all right. I'm interested in what rubbish comes out of his mouth next. It's very entertaining. But if you mean interested in going out with him … no chance. He's really not my type.'

'But he's gorgeous.'

'I admit he's easier on the eye than say, Father Ted or Old Don, but he has the personality of a turnip.'

Amy looked crestfallen. 'He's just a little nervous around you, that's all. It's because you're kind of….'

'Kind of…?'

Amy stuffed another lump of chicken into her mouth, then immediately coughed. 'Hot. Hot! Hot hot hot!'

'I hope you're not talking about me,' Jennifer said, handing Amy a glass of water.

Amy erupted into a fit of coughing while she intermittently forced the water down. Jennifer was mildly impressed how little of it spilled on the floor, which was conveniently patterned in reds and oranges in case of just such an event.

Amy, surviving the spice overload, flapped a hand in front of her face and shook her head. 'No, I meant … while I wouldn't say you were hot … I mean, if I played for the other team I might think you were, but … you're just kind of mildly gorgeous. For a teacher, I mean. It's kind of a standard issue that teachers have to be dogs, isn't it?'

'Do they? I don't remember seeing that on the application.' Jennifer smiled. '"Must be a dog".'

'It's in the small print,' Amy insisted. 'The very small print. The small print that's between the lines that you can't actually read. You have to be a dog otherwise the kids will get the horn and it'll cause problems.'

Jennifer, starting to wish she'd stayed home after all, winced. 'Uh, this is a primary school? Most of them are several years off puberty yet.' She grinned. 'So, what you're saying is that I'm not a dog.'

Amy gave a frustrated sigh. 'This is so much easier with beer. I'm saying that when the options are Maud on reception or Vicky the school councillor who has that gippy eye, or well, me, it's obvious that Rick's going to be aiming for you like one of Shop's arrows.'

'Um, Shop? Who's Shop?'

Amy shook her head. 'Do I have to explain everything? Shop. You know, Downton Abbey? Friar Tuck? Tuck Shop?'

'Ah … I get it.'

'That's one of mine. Do you think Rick will be impressed?'

Jennifer shrugged and gave Amy what she hoped was a supportive smile. 'He might.'

Amy grinned, then stuffed an enormous piece of naan bread into her mouth, as though afraid the family loading food on to their plates nearby might mistake Amy and Jennifer's table as part of the buffet.

'So,' she mumbled through a mouthful of bread, 'Didn't you say you wanted to talk to me about something?'

Jennifer smiled. 'Oh, it was nothing. Just about the teachers' play, that's all.'

11

SIDEWAYS PICKS

'So, you think you can just like, do your colouring and ignore me? You'll get a dead arm in a minute—'

Gavin Gordon stood over Matthew Bridges' table with one little fist raised, while the tiny boy's hands covered over a partially coloured picture of a Roman legionnaire. Spotting the potential situation early, Jennifer left the Jarder twins to finish their poster on Ancient Egypt and quickly slid between the two boys.

'No, Matthew does not want a dead arm,' she said, ducking down to get into Gavin's eyeline. The stocky, slightly overweight boy had a sour look on his face, his eyes a little gummy, not unintelligent but overwhelmed by a need to commit violence.

'Gavin, can I have a word with you outside for a moment?' Jennifer asked.

'I didn't do nothing,' Gavin protested. 'I was just saying.'

'Come with me.'

Head bowed, Gavin followed Jennifer out into the corridor, no doubt expecting yet another dressing down.

Having had to keep him back at lunchtime two days in a row last week, Jennifer was pleased that today she had something different to say.

'Gavin … I need to ask you something important.'

'I didn't hit him.'

'I know you didn't. I was watching you. This isn't about that. This is about the harvest festival.'

Gavin just nodded and stared sullenly at the floor, perhaps expecting to be told he was to be excluded. She knew how much that would hurt him, as despite his bluster and regular threats of violence against other children, the poster he had made for their class's wall display was as good as anyone's. Although, to be fair, he'd had a couple of extra lunchtimes to work on it, Jennifer remembered with a smile.

'Our class is in charge of the cake stall this year,' she said, as Gavin looked up at her, his face defiant, ready to protest any attempt at exclusion. 'And … we need a manager. Someone to coordinate all the other pupils. The manager must make sure everyone who's family is able to —and we'll talk about that—has provided a cake, then decide pricing, organise who's going to work behind the counter, that kind of thing.'

Gavin continued to stare at her, the penny yet to drop.

'And I've decided that this year you will be the manager.'

Gavin's eyes widened. 'Me?'

'Yes, you. You, Gavin.'

'But what about Bridges, or that swot Vickers? He always does stuff like this.'

'I have plenty of other duties that need to be allocated. But for this duty, I've chosen you.'

'No way.'

'Are you pleased?'

Gavin just shrugged.

'I'm afraid it'll mean you'll need to sit with me for a few minutes on some lunchtimes to go over the plans, but it'll only be for a few minutes, and it's not as a punishment. It's just that managers have certain duties.'

'And I get to pick my workers? I bet Lemon would do it—'

'Within reason. I think Paul Lemon would be better suited to car park duty. But we can discuss it. So … what do you say?'

Gavin gave her a beaming smile, and from the tone of his voice, Jennifer could tell he was happy. 'Yeah. Go on then.'

~

'YOU'RE OUT OF YOUR MIND.'

Rick stood by the coffee machine, a mug in his hand with a Starbucks individual filter poking out of the top. The way he drank his coffee with the filter still in the cup irked Jennifer no end, to the point where she hoped one day it would flop out while he was taking a sip and upend itself down his shirt.

'I think it was inspirational,' Amy said from her desk, where she was lining rubbers up against a ruler and then cutting the smudged edges off with a Stanley knife. 'It might be just what that boy needs.'

'Well, say goodbye to your class getting the prize for best stall,' Rick said. 'You let that idiot Gordon be in charge and you'll be lucky if any of the cakes make it as far as the stall. He'll be selling them outside the arcade on the high street to raise money for his vapes.'

'I'm pretty sure he doesn't vape,' Jennifer said.

'Give him time.'

'I'm hoping the extra responsibility will be the making of him,' Jennifer said. 'Since his dad left he's had nothing to focus his frustration on.'

Rick took a sip of his coffee, then upended the leftover filter straight into the rubbish bin, coffee splashing down the plastic sides. 'Right, I'd better stop gasbagging with you two. My class has games next.'

'Good luck!' Amy said in a titter that was just a little too high-pitched to sound normal.

'Come join us if you fancy a couple of extra laps,' he said. 'Not going to burn off breakfast watching DVDs about wildlife.'

'Actually, we're going on a nature walk,' Amy said. 'Down to Sycamore Park and back.'

'Well, watch out for hunters,' Rick said with a smirk, before setting his unwashed cup in the sink and heading out.

'I have no idea what you see in him,' Jennifer said. 'Convicts have better manners.'

Amy, who was staring forlornly at the door just closing behind Rick, sighed. 'I'm really not quite sure what it is,' she said. 'I think, deep inside, he kind of likes me too, because if he didn't he would just ignore me, wouldn't he?'

'You think he rips on you because he secretly likes you?' Jennifer shrugged. 'It's not impossible. I wouldn't get your hopes up, though. And I imagine he's like one of those supermarket cake counters—the cakes look good on the outside, but on the inside, they're hollow and worthless.'

'I think you have trust issues,' Amy said.

'I—'

The bell rang. Jennifer just flashed Amy a smile and headed off to class, dodging the children coming in from break as they raced down the corridors, bouncing off each other like dodgem cars.

By the time she got to the classroom, several of the kids were already there, standing around, chatting or teasing each other, playing tabletop games or generally mucking about. Jennifer was about to call for order when Matthew Bridges came in, supported on each side by the Jarder twins. His face was scrunched up like an old towel, one trouser leg pulled up to reveal a nasty graze on his knee.

'I didn't do nothing!' Gavin Gordon snapped, as two other boys herded him in through the door.

'You pushed him!' Rachel Low snapped, aiming a swipe at Gavin's face which Jennifer had to move quickly to intercept.

'No, I didn't, he tripped!'

'Yes, you did!'

Jennifer tried to tend to a sobbing Matthew while steering the other kids to their seats. In the end, she instructed the Jarder twins to take Matthew to the school nurse, before putting on a DVD while she took Gavin out into the corridor.

'Okay,' she said, squatting down in front of him. 'No one else is here. Don't lie to me, because I'll know. I used to be a spy.'

At this attempt at humour, there was a brief curl at the edge of Gavin's lips, but it was gone quickly enough to convince Jennifer not just of Gavin's guilt, but also his remorse.

'You pushed him, didn't you?'

Gavin nodded. 'But I didn't mean to. We were playing football and he just got in the way. I was trying to get to the ball. I didn't even know it was Bridges until he started screaming like a girl.'

At moments like this, Jennifer could understand why so many teachers had stress issues. She closed her eyes and took a deep breath. It would be easy to ball him out, perhaps channel a little of her own frustration into a vicious tongue-lashing, but she was trying to improve the situation, not push Gavin further along one of Greg Downton's life paths.

'I'll talk to him and explain,' Jennifer said. 'I want you to try to be more careful. Matthew's a lot smaller than you.'

'He just kind of bounced off.'

Jennifer had to suppress a smile of her own as she imagined the scene in her mind. Gavin wasn't a bad kid, but he was probably twice Matthew's weight and boisterous. Most kids would bounce off him.

'Look, be more careful. I'm not going to keep you behind or punish you, but I want you to promise me that you'll try harder. I expect more from my chief of staff.'

Gavin's eyes widened. 'So you're not going to pick someone else?'

Jennifer shook her head. 'No. I've picked you, and I'm sticking with you, unless you do something really bad, like burn down the school. Please don't do that.'

Gavin's face broke into a wide smile. 'I'll say sorry to Matthew, I promise. Thanks, Miss. Thanks.'

Jennifer nodded. 'Please, please don't make me regret this,' she said.

12

HEART TO HEART

'I MISSED YOU,' Jennifer said, peering around the door of the Oak Leaf Café. Angela, wiping a table near the window, looked up and smiled.

'There you are, my dear. Did you have a good day at work? How are the preparations for the festival going?'

Jennifer came in and closed the door against a chilly breeze blowing through Sycamore Park.

'Well, on Monday I appointed the class bully as the head of our class's cake stand. By lunchtime he had sent the class weakling to the nurse's room. In the afternoon, one of the two identical twins was sick in the classroom. I got her name wrong and only made things worse because the other one started crying. Yesterday, two kids got in a fight over a pack of crayons and one ended up with a suspension warning. Then, this morning, the kid I picked as head of staff overturned a flower pot on the table of a group of girls. It's been a little testing, to say the least.'

Angela looked up at the clock. 'It's nearly six. Too early for wine? I've not had a customer all day, so I've done my pies for the week already. I was actually thinking of closing early and maybe go and see a movie or something. I couldn't interest you, could I?'

'I'd love to, but I need to get back and take Bonky out before it gets too cold.'

Angela smiled. 'Just the one glass, then?'

'Just the one.'

'Oh, and I could do with a guinea pig for a couple of new culinary ideas,' Angela said. 'Do you have room for a sweet potato stew and some pumpkin and walnut pie?'

Jennifer grinned. 'I could force a little down, I suppose.'

Angela clapped her hands together. 'Great. I'll rustle some up. I've not eaten yet this evening, so I'll join you, if it's okay. In fact, it looks like it's going to rain, so I might as well turn the closed sign around.'

Angela bustled off into the kitchen, refusing Jennifer's offer to help, then reappeared a few minutes later with two steaming bowls of stew, a side salad, and a plate of freshly baked bread rolls. Jennifer's mouth was watering, but as Angela sat down she lifted an eyebrow and said, 'I saw Tom this morning.'

Jennifer shifted uncomfortably on her seat. 'Oh?'

'He said to tell you that Francis will be fine. It was a dislocation, not a break, so he'll be back on the water within a couple of weeks.'

'Oh, that's good news.'

'And he also said to tell you that the council has approved the use of the park for Brentwell Primary's harvest festival.'

Jennifer clapped her hands together. 'Fantastic! I'll tell the school tomorrow.'

'He said someone will call them anyway to make sure they know it's official.'

'Great.'

'And he also said he hopes to see you around again sometime.'

'Oh, well, I hope so too.'

Angela narrowed her eyes. 'Did something happen between you two? He looked a little crestfallen.'

'I ... I ... I just ... found myself in a situation that I felt uncomfortable with. Tom seems like a lovely guy, it's just....'

'Something happened to you before you came here, didn't it?' Angela said. 'I could tell from the first time I met you. You were so guarded about anything personal. I know your dog's favourite brand of food but I don't even know where you're from.'

'South Gloucestershire,' Jennifer blurted. 'Originally.'

Angela stood up. 'I almost forgot the wine. I'll be just right back. Then we can have a heart to heart.'

Jennifer was tempted to do a runner while Angela was in the kitchen, but the food was too good, it looked too chilly outside, and after her failed attempt to talk to Amy at the weekend, it was perhaps about time to get her thoughts off her chest.

'Here we are,' Angela said, coming back and setting two glasses of red wine on the table, before sitting back down. 'Cheers to damaged friends.'

Jennifer lifted an eyebrow as they clinked glasses. 'You too?'

Angela smiled. 'Divorced. Been over ten years now, so I'm all good. I got the café and the flat upstairs, he got the rest.' She shrugged. 'It happens. We'd grown apart. He was older, about to retire, and wanted to move overseas. I stalked him on Facebook a couple of years ago and he was out in New Zealand.'

'What about ... um—'

'Children?' Angela shook her head and sighed. 'It

didn't happen. We wanted them, but for one reason or other … it just never came to pass. Jonathan and I have no ties except the years we spent together. The memories are good, and perhaps in other circumstances … but my life is here. This is my home. Did you know it's rumoured that one of my ancestors planted Big Gerry? Or at least was at the planting ceremony.' She smiled. 'I kind of consider myself to be that tree's protector.'

'I'm sure if he could speak, he'd tell you how pleased he was,' Jennifer said.

Angela leaned back and sipped her wine. 'So. Your turn.'

'Ah … I'm not sure where to start.'

'At the beginning. Or in the middle, if that makes a better place.'

'I was with someone before I came here. Mark.' Jennifer paused. It sounded strange to say his name out loud after so long. 'We were living together in Dottingham.'

'Oh, I know it. Horrible little place. Best thing about it is the motorway entrance ramp on the way out.'

'It's not that bad,' Jennifer said, struggling to recall anything she had actually liked about it. Perhaps Angela was right.

'So, Mark.'

'Yes, ah … we were living together, had been for a couple of years. We met in a bar in town. He was a stock-broker. Lots of money. He drove a Tesla, shopped at Waitrose—'

'There's a Waitrose in Dottingham now?'

'No, when he was off on business trips. He said he hated the shops in Dottingham. Too many poor people.'

'Was he having an affair?'

'Not that I know of.'

'Did he—'

'No! He never touched me. He was always polite, treated me well, bought me whatever I wanted, it's just….'

'He wasn't really there.'

Jennifer nodded. 'That's it in a nutshell.'

'He looked through you, like he was living in a different world, and you were only part in it?'

'How did you know?'

'Jonathan was the same near the end. That's why I let him go.'

Jennifer sighed. 'It sounds like you might understand.'

'Try me.'

Jennifer took a sip of her wine. 'At first I thought he was great. We could do whatever we wanted, go where we liked. But after we'd been together a while, it seemed like he'd have two business trips for every day we had together, and soon all he did was go on business trips. Nights he met clients, weekends he went off to play golf. Sometimes he'd be gone all week. And when he was there, he'd talk at me, not to me. He never asked me how I was, what I'd been doing. I left no impression on him. We had a maid so I didn't need to clean, and we had home food deliveries so I didn't even need to cook. Just open the packets, eat, throw away.' She flapped her hands, then snatched up her wine and took a long swallow. 'I worked in the local school, but he always dismissed what I did as irrelevant. Told me if it was hard I should just quit, stay at home. He said the pets would keep me company. James was my grandmother's cat, and I took him in when she passed. Bonky, Mark gave me for my birthday. Said I needed a reason to get out of the house on weekends.' She realised she was crying. 'I'd hoped having a boyfriend might have been reason enough, but he was only there one weekend every couple of months.'

Angela fished into her pocket for a tissue and handed it to Jennifer, who took it with a grateful smile. 'So you pulled the plug on the relationship?' Angela said.

'I tried to talk to him a dozen times,' Jennifer said, 'but it was one-way traffic. He never seemed to be listening. In the end I started to make plans. I quit my job, got a new one, moved my stuff out bit by bit and then left completely one weekend while he was over in France on a golfing holiday. I left him a note to say I'd gone, and not to try to contact me.'

'Does he know where you are?'

'No one knows where I am. If he comes after me, I know I'll break and go back. He'll say what he needs to say, and I'll be taken in by it, and I'll go back with him, hoping things will be different. Then they won't be, and I'll be back at square one. You see, despite everything that our relationship had become, I still loved him. I love him now, I just wanted to have my life back.'

'I won't ham on any silly quotes,' Angela said, 'but it's true what they say. Sometimes you can love someone but not fit with them. It's the way of the world. And really, there's no one true person for anyone, despite what the telly might have you believe. There's a whole host of people who'd line up just fine. You just need to do a little more window shopping.'

'I'm too tired. It sucked the life out of me to leave Mark. I feel like a zombie most of the time. I don't like being at home alone because I get tempted to call him, and the doubts start to creep in. The only thing that's keeping me going is the school, and this café, and well, you.'

Angela smiled. 'If you want me to fill your time with some evening and weekend shifts at the café, just let me know,' she said. 'I'd love someone to have a natter with on a quiet day.'

Jennifer laughed. 'I'll give it some thought.'

'So what are you going to do? I can tell you right now, that one hundred percent you did the right thing, and that the more time that passes, the better you'll feel about it. Plus, you're still young. Plenty of time left to find someone else, if that's what you want.'

Jennifer shrugged. 'I'm just not sure what I'm after right now. With Mark I felt like I'd become invisible, and all I really want is to be part of the world again. I mean, Tom seems nice, but I just can't do relationships right now.'

'Well, let's help you concentrate on the things you *can* do. There's getting your class ready, and there's helping with your teachers' drama ... and there's the protest on Saturday morning.'

'What protest?'

'It's against the council's plan to cut down Big Gerry. I trust you'll be there?'

Jennifer stared, openmouthed. 'Uh ... with bells on.'

Angela clapped her hands together, then picked up the bottle of wine from where she'd put it on the adjacent table. 'Great. And please bring anyone who you think might be interested. The more the merrier. Right, let's just top these up and then we'll eat. It still counts as the same glass if you haven't completely finished it.'

13

PROGRESS

'IT WASN'T ME, MISS!'

Jennifer closed her eyes for a second to regain her composure, then snapped them open, trying to do her best angry teacher face, even if she knew deep down there was no bite behind her pseudo-bark.

'Gavin, please just pick them up and hand them out as I asked you. This is important.'

'It wasn't me,' Gavin protested, as he scowled and bent down to scoop up the parents' letters Jennifer had hastily typed out and printed at lunchtime. 'It was that swot Vickers. He tripped me.'

'I don't care,' she said, as the accused Vickers started to protest. 'Please just hand out the letters.'

'It's not fair,' Gavin grumbled, but at least he finally began to carry out the order, distributing the letters among the kids.

'Now, take these letters home and give them to your parents,' Jennifer said.

'"Save Big Gerry"' Paul Lemon read out in a loud, mocking voice, to laughter from the other boys on his table. 'What's Big Gerry? An elephant?'

'A tree, Paul,' Jennifer said through gritted teeth. 'A very old, important tree.'

'Can't they grow a new one?'

'Just ... give the letter to your parents.'

With an emphatic groan, Paul stuffed the letter into his bag.

'Okay, coats on, everyone, please. It's getting cold out there.'

Nothing felt better than watching her pupils leave on a Friday afternoon. Several of the teachers had already planned to go to the pub, and the offer was extremely tempting. As Jennifer watched the last bus leave, however, she turned to see Greg Downton walking across the car park towards her, a sheet of paper in his hand.

'Um, Miss Stevens, a word, please.'

'Yes?'

'Is this yours?'

He held up her original print of the letter and flapped it about. Jennifer groaned; she must have left it on the photocopier.

'You do know, don't you, that pushing your ... activism on to the kids isn't really appropriate?'

Jennifer felt her cheeks burning. Amy had suggested it was a good idea, but Jennifer had neglected to run it by the Church first.

'It isn't activism, it's just a notice. There's no obligation to do anything. And anyway, it's a good cause. That tree is four hundred years old.'

'About time they planted a new one, then.'

'But what about the harvest festival? If they decide to cut down the tree, they'll have their crews in there at the same time. It'll be so noisy.'

'Well, we should have had it at the Community Centre on Porter Street, shouldn't we?'

Downton was clearly still stewing. After the council had agreed to relocating the school festival to Sycamore Park, he had put it to a vote among the teachers. Only Maud, himself and Old Don Jones had voted against. Amy, bouncing like a rubber ball, had stuck up two hands, because, 'One's for Clara! She'd have loved the festival to be in Sycamore Park! It was her second favorite place after her classroom!'

Downton, who still had the final say, had reluctantly agreed to the relocation.

'I think the school should have more interest in community events,' Jennifer said, sensing a weakening of Downton's exoskeleton. 'It's good for the kids to have more awareness of the world around them.'

'Well, run it past me first next time,' Downton said. Grumbling under his breath, he stuffed his hands into his pockets and headed for the staffroom.

IN THE END, Jennifer declined the offer of a drink in the pub, preferring to go down to the high street to do a little food shopping for the weekend. Trying to convince herself she wasn't on some sort of reconnaissance mission, she tried really hard not to be near to the museum just as it closed, pretending to browse the listings in an estate agent window as the doors opened and Gavin Gordon's mum came out, still wearing her staff uniform, a bag over her shoulder.

'Oh, hi there,' Marlie said, spotting Jennifer. 'It's Miss Stevens, isn't it?'

'Oh, ah … hi. I was just doing some dreaming. Houses aren't cheap around here, are they?'

'They're not cheap anywhere anymore,' Marlie said with a sad smile. 'Even rent is through the roof. We're barely hanging on.'

'It's nice that I've bumped into you,' Jennifer said. She thought about the bag of flour Gavin had upended over the Jarder twins in home economics class and wondered how she would explain it. 'I—'

'Oh, is it about Gavin?' Marlie's face brightened. 'I don't know how you do it, but he's a different person since you put him in charge of your class's cake stall. It's all he talks about. Instead of tearing about the house, he's been drawing out all these plans, making price lists … I've never seen anything like it.'

Jennifer had to force herself to speak. 'Um … really?'

'And it's Miss Stevens this, Miss Stevens, that. All the time.' Marlie took hold of Jennifer's hands. 'I'd like to thank you for the positive effect you're having on my son.' Then, quickly checking her watch, she added, 'I have to go. I have to run to Tesco then get to the youth club to pick Gavin up before six.' She sighed. 'It's tough … without his dad.'

Jennifer gave a sympathetic smile. 'You're doing your best. That's the most important thing.'

Marlie nodded. 'Thank you,' she said again.

As Jennifer watched her hurry away, she wondered how she could get Gavin to translate his newfound home attitude to the classroom, before Downton decided to expel him. It had taken a white lie—blaming it on a slip—to get him off a week's detention for the flour incident, and Gavin was already an honorary recipient of Downton's favourite label—prison-bound.

It wouldn't be easy, but as Jennifer found herself

growing back into the person so long suppressed by Mark's presence, it felt less of a worry, and more of a challenge.

She glanced at her watch. Five thirty.

The food shopping could wait until tomorrow. Just enough time to run home, take Bonky out for a walk, then make a banner for tomorrow's protest.

14

THE PROTEST MARCH

'SAVE BIG GERRY!' Amy shouted, flapping a Union Jack flag in the air, then giving a jubilant whoop. Then, turning to Jennifer, she whispered, 'Which tree is it again?'

'The big one.'

'The leaning one?'

'Yes.'

Amy pouted. 'It does look a bit wonky.'

'We're not against them giving it a little trim,' Jennifer said. 'We just don't want them cutting it down completely.'

She looked around the group who had assembled on this chilly Saturday morning. A scattering of mostly older people in woolly hats and thick coats, everyone looked defiantly unhappy except Pete Markham, who had set up his van on the edge of the courtyard and was doing a roaring trade in burgers and hot coffee. Amy, who had been eyeing the van since her arrival, was already two coffees and a double egg bap deep, and looked keen to get started on brunch, even with the sun barely up.

'If they just propped it up with a stick or something,

that would be okay,' Amy said, blowing on her hands as she hopped from foot to foot.

'That's the hope, but Angela said it would cost more than just cutting it down.'

'They do like to cut corners, these councils,' Amy said. 'Very big ones.' Raising a hand into the air, she shouted, 'Don't cut corners, or trees!'

'Good morning!' came Angela's spritely voice. Jennifer turned to see her friend walking across the courtyard in a thick puffer jacket, a banner from her shoulder to her waist that read Save Big Gerry in big orange marker pen letters.

'Thanks for coming,' she said to Jennifer and Amy. 'They'll get our message before the day is out, that's for sure.'

'Are the council actually here?' Jennifer asked.

'Not yet, but we've got the local news showing up in half an hour. We're hoping a few more people will come by then, too. Pad out the numbers.'

Amy looked at Jennifer. 'It's an excuse to call Rick. Should I do it?'

Jennifer shrugged. 'Won't he be hungover?'

'Probably, but I never have a reason to call him. It's a good excuse, isn't it?'

'Go on, then.'

Amy took out her phone and pulled up a number. 'I got it off the staff contacts list. Do you think that counts as stalking?'

'Ah … I think you're okay.'

'Can you speak? Can you speak?' Amy gasped, jumping up and down, holding the phone out to Jennifer as beside her, Angela laughed.

'Hi, Rick,' Jennifer said, trying to suppress a groan as she rolled her eyes at Amy. 'I'm really sorry about this, but—'

'Oh, you're after Rick, are you?' came a woman's voice from the other end of the line. Jennifer's mouth clamped shut. 'I'm afraid he's still in bed. Would you like me to wake him for you? Who is this?'

Jennifer's cheeks burned. The woman sounded tired, as though a night on the tiles with Rick must have exhausted her, whoever she was. 'Ah … it's just Jennifer from work,' she stammered. 'Nothing that can't wait until Monday.'

'Oh, that's all right. I'll let him know you called.'

'Thanks.'

The other end of the line went dead as though Jennifer's implication in some charade had been uncovered. She handed the phone back to Amy then wiped the sweat off her palm on to her shirt.

'I'm sorry,' she said. 'Rick's … ah … busy. He's still … in bed.'

Amy looked heartbroken but gave a stoic little shrug. 'Ah, well. He does work hard. His class are terrors, aren't they?'

Only because he lets them get away with everything while he checks his Tinder profile under the desk, Jennifer, who had once taken a peak in through Rick's classroom window while on the way back from a P.E. class with her kids, wanted to say. Instead, she just said, 'It must be hard.'

'Save Big Gerry!' Amy shouted, fist pumping into the air, her voice loud enough to make Jennifer step back and almost trip over a raised section of paving. Then, turning to Jennifer, Amy smirked and said, 'Got to channel the energy, haven't you?'

'I suppose. Save Big Gerry.'

'Save Big Gerry!'

Jennifer was about to attempt to outdo Amy's shout when she saw a familiar figure moving through the crowd. Tom looked like he'd just come out of a potting shed, wearing a tatty waxed jacket, jeans, and a faded cap he could have pulled out of a rubbish bin. Despite what looked like an obvious attempt to dress down, his sheer size and the angles of his face made Jennifer's stomach ache. She looked away, hoping he wouldn't see her, but too late, he had caught her eye. He smiled and wandered over.

'Thanks for coming down,' he said. 'It's a pretty good showing.'

'It looks like the tree means a lot to people,' Jennifer said, wishing she had a way with wit or charm, instead of sounding like a middle-pages newspaper column. 'And, ah, sorry about the other night.'

Tom smiled again. 'It's quite all right. Not the circumstances for a first proper meeting, really, was it? Any time you'd like to stop by, I've always got the kettle on in my little shack over there. It's not much, but it's enough.'

'Thanks, I will.'

Tom looked about to say something else, but instead just patted her on the forearm, then excused himself to mingle among the crowd. Jennifer turned as someone tugged on her arm.

'Who's the hunk?' Amy gasped, both hands clutching folds in Jennifer's sleeve and working them up and down as though she were trying to shake a dead animal back into life. 'Oh. My. God. I'm practically hyperventilating. How did you find a way to speak?'

'That's Tom Reynolds,' Jennifer said. 'He's the park caretaker.'

'And the next Batman, with pecs like that,' Amy said, making Jennifer cringe. 'Has he taken you for a workout?'

'Ah … what kind of workout?'

Amy, whose original question had perhaps been quite innocent, suddenly narrowed her eyes. 'Oh, I didn't mean

… oh, you haven't! Jennifer … no wonder you look so tired at work.'

'No! I haven't! We're just friends. Barely even that. I mean, he seems to live in a shed in the park. I can't—'

'It's probably a love dungeon.'

'It was full of wheelbarrows and trellises.'

Amy's eyes twinkled. 'Tools for love.'

'I don't know what twisted world you live in, but let's go and grab a couple more coffees before Pete sells out.'

'Sure.'

They headed over to the burger van. Pete Markham gave them a salute, then grinned. 'Half price for anyone fighting the good fight for Big Gerry's justice,' he said, then turned and tapped a little transistor radio behind him. 'The council are on their way, in full riot gear.'

'Really?'

Pete grinned. 'Not quite. But Regina Clover is here.'

'Oh, what a pretty name,' Amy said.

Pete grimaced. 'I just sold her an egg roll. Full price, of course. You'll be able to find her by following the trail of dead grass, where the birds no longer sing.'

'She's that bad?'

'She transferred from the taxation department last year into environmental management. Allegedly her plan is to have Big Gerry sliced up to make expensive furniture for the kind of rich people who would only ever buy something from Brentwell if it was on the internet. Luckily, she's only one of three councillors in the environmental management department, so we only have to convince the other two.'

'Hallelujah for democracy!' Amy shouted, punching the air again.

'Two coffees, please,' Jennifer said. 'We need our fuel before we resume our vigil.'

'Coming right up.'

They got their coffees and headed back over to the protest. A few more people had shown up. Jennifer was delighted to see the Jarder twins with their dad, Ron, both girls with A4 sheets of paper with pictures of Big Gerry taped to the fronts of their coats. And also there, much to Jennifer's surprise, was Gavin Gordon with Marlie beside him. He was carrying a wooden sign with All Trees Matter written on it in black marker pen, with a scribbled picture of a tree underneath. He gave Jennifer a shy glance, before throwing a glare at the Jarder twins, as though to warn them not to say anything at school. With her dad's back turned to talk to someone he knew, Kelly Jarder put a finger to her nose and stuck out her tongue.

'Good to see the kids getting involved,' Amy said. 'Isn't it—Oh. My. God. I don't believe it. You'll never guess who's here!'

Before Jennifer could turn around, Amy had reached up and slapped hands that smelled of egg over Jennifer's eyes. 'What are you doing?'

'Guess, guess, guess!'

'Rick?'

'No!'

'Old Don Jones?'

'*No!*'

'Michael Jackson?'

'No, no, no! *Look!*'

She pulled her hands away and pointed. Jennifer stared. Michael Jackson would have been less of a surprise. Striding through the gates with a scarf tied around his neck and a woolly hat pulled down to his eyebrows, was Greg Downton.

'Well, perhaps he's come to offer Big Gerry some

divine intervention,' Amy said. 'Oh, God, that was good. And, woah, there I go again!'

Downton spotted them, gave them a sour nod, and wandered over. 'So, this is what you do with your free time, is it? I'll have to campaign harder for weekend classes.'

'Are you here to support Big Gerry, Greg?'

Downton shrugged. 'Cut it down for all I care. I just wanted to see where the festival's going to be held. I come down here and it's mayhem. So many tree huggers I'm surprised the thing doesn't fall down.'

'It's not really a hug on a tree that big, though is it?' Amy said. 'I mean, your hands can't touch.'

'Is that the definition of a hug, is it?' Jennifer said. 'Your hands have to touch on the other side?'

'Of course it is. Otherwise it's just an embrace. So technically, we'd be tree embracers.'

'You women are off your nuts,' Downton said. 'I suppose that's what standing out in this cold does to you. Fries your brain.'

Angela came squeezing through the crowd and patted Jennifer on the shoulder. She gave Greg and Amy a quick smile and then said, 'Regina's going to speak to the crowd. This should be interesting.'

Over by Big Gerry, Tom had set up a small microphone and amplifier. He helped Regina Clover to stand on a bench right in front of the great tree's trunk. Regina, a woman who looked well past retirement age and pretty angry about it into the bargain, grumbled about the bench's unevenness before realising the microphone was already switch on. Then, giving a little cough, she looked up at the crowd.

'Thank you for coming,' she said. 'It's much appreciated that you all showed up, but what's more important is how many of Brentwell's residents didn't show up. Most of them, actually.'

'They've got to pay their taxes!' someone shouted.

'I can tell how much the few of you here love this old lump of collapsing wood,' Regina continued, 'but unfortunately times change. While it will be put to a vote, because this is, of course—' she gave a long sigh, '—a democracy, don't expect to see this tree come spring.' She gave a little laugh as people booed.

'Nice fur coat, Cruella!' someone else shouted.

'Look on the literal bright side,' Regina continued. 'You'll get a lot more sunlight once this monstrosity is gone.'

As more people booed and hissed, she climbed down from the bench, scowled at the crowd, then walked off in the direction of the north entrance.

Angela grimaced. 'Short and sour, as ever,' she said.

'Like a lemon biscuit!' Amy said.

Tom wandered over, as the first people began to disperse. 'Well, that was interesting,' he said. 'Looks like she's got her decision set in stone. We'll have to do more to convince the other two.'

'And Rome fell,' Downton said, turning to Jennifer and Amy. 'I'll see you two on Monday. Don't let your activism get in the way of your teaching. If I spot any camouflage paint or bumper stickers, you'll be in my office for a ticking off.'

As he wandered away through the crowd, Angela clapped her hands together. 'Who's up for a slice of maple and apple cake and a war council in the café?'

'Me, me, me!' Amy shouted.

Jennifer looked at Tom, who smiled and shrugged.

'Come on, then,' Jennifer said, just as the first drops of rain began to fall.

15

PHILOSOPHY

JENNIFER WOKE on Sunday to find Bonky sleeping under one arm and James under the other. As she shifted, the dog just rolled over, one ear flopping over his face, while the cat gave her a playful bat with his paw before jumping down and ambling over to his regular window seat.

The skies were clear, sunlight shining in through the window. Jennifer got up and wandered into the kitchen to make breakfast, still trying to make sense of how a morning protest had turned into an all-day event centred at first around Angela's café, and then the entire community as they first printed and then distributed leaflets asking local residents to show their support for Big Gerry by contacting the council. Then followed an attempted late afternoon picnic, only for the rain to come rolling in to spoil it in true autumn style, and a relocation back to the café.

And through it all, Jennifer had somehow managed to resist both telling Amy that she had spoken to a woman at Rick's house, and falling in love with Tom.

She just couldn't go there. The underlying snob part of

her—the rule that she should always aim for someone higher in station than herself drilled into her by her mother throughout her teenage years—felt reluctant to get involved with a man who worked as a glorified gardener, while the moral part of her felt it inappropriate, and the sensitive part just wasn't ready. It had barely been a couple of months since she had left Mark, and she just couldn't go there again.

Even if Tom really had the nicest of smiles.

Focusing her attention elsewhere seemed the most appropriate thing to do, so she busied herself for an hour trying to find Bonky's vaccination certificates, sure he was due for one soon, only to find that it didn't need doing until January. And then there was setting up the coffee table she had bought just before moving in, but that only took half an hour, and then it wasn't even lunchtime and she couldn't think of anything to do except stare at her phone and maybe stalk Mark on social media.

She had deleted all of her own that she could, and blocked him on the others she wanted to keep, but he hadn't done any such thing to her. His Facebook profile came up as public, even though they were no longer friends. Jennifer hesitated just a moment before clicking and quickly scrolling down, hoping perhaps for some misery, a few heartbroken posts, a plea perhaps that he could get back together with the ex who had run out on him.

She didn't have to look far, however, to have her worst fears confirmed. The first new photo was of some exotic golf course with palm trees along one side of the fairway and a distant seascape suggesting it was somewhere over-seas. Mark's only comment was "Next on the list!" to which a handful of his golfing mates had replied with various comments in agreement. None seemed perceptive enough to mention where exactly it was. The date was just a week before, but when Jennifer scrolled past, the next picture hit her like a falling piano.

Mark's face in close-up, with a woman's pressed so tightly against it that was as though they were waiting for glue to set. Both wore beaming smiles, their faces nearly blemish free, a sign of early nights and juicers and more fantastic sex than Jennifer could imagine from a man who had largely left her to sleep alone once their initial honeymoon period had faded.

The only comment was a fat red heart that Jennifer wished she could reach into her phone and pop with a virtual needle.

Even worse was that the woman was familiar: Heather Wilton, a colleague at Mark's whatever-he-does company, whom Mark had occasionally name-dropped in a casual manner, and whom Jennifer had even met at a couple of social events. Worse was that the girl was as pleasant and personable as it was possible for a rival to be, completely impossible to dislike, harmless yet interesting, polite yet full of life, dressed down yet quietly beautiful.

The comments, those which contained words rather than lines of emoticons and nausea-inducing kisses or hearts, were all congratulatory, praising a relationship now made official.

Jennifer cleared her phone's screen and narrowly resisted throwing it against the nearest wall.

Then, grabbing a bottle of water, because that was all she could find in her fridge which wouldn't require any preparation effort, she sat down on the sofa to cry.

It wasn't that he had moved on. She was happy for him. It was that the hole her absence from his life had left had been so quickly and efficiently filled and raked over it was as though she had never existed at all.

Bonky jumped up on the sofa to join her in her misery.

'Who am I, Bonky?' she said, patting the little dog on the back. 'Who on earth am I?'

Bonky just gave a little bark, ready for his morning walk.

OAK LEAF CAFÉ was shut so Jennifer got a coffee from Pete's van and led Bonky over to Tom's shack, a mischievous part of her wanting to do something reckless to overcome her current unbearable lightness, but God or fate or karma wasn't biting and the shack was locked up and quiet, Tom nowhere to be seen. Instead she wandered aimlessly through Sycamore Park, letting Bonky chase the pigeons, watching the joggers and the other dog walkers, a group of teenagers practicing a dance routine outside the theatre, a young couple leaning on each others' shoulders on a bench, an old man picking around in a flowerbed, perhaps looking for something he had lost.

The sun was shining, the air crisp and cool, but Jennifer couldn't overcome the feeling that she should be *doing* something, moving her life forward, improving herself, changing the world. She led Bonky off the slope, up to the top of the grassy knoll from where she could see all corners of the park: the playground, the theatre and the library, the duck pond, the crazy paving courtyard over which Big Gerry resided, the south entrance and Pete's burger van, the north where Angela's café stood closed. She felt at the centre of a world; whether it was *her* world, she couldn't be sure. But letting Bonky nose around in the grass, she lay back, staring up at the clear blue sky, and let the revolving machine beneath her spin on.

It was sometime later when she opened her eyes to find

a silhouette standing above her, backlit by the noon sun.

'Hello, dear,' came Angela's kind voice. 'I thought I recognised the soles of your shoes from my window. Are you in the middle of a crisis or is this some new form of meditation?'

Jennifer sat up. Bonky was curled up between her knees, panting in Angela's general direction.

'Definitely a crisis,' Jennifer said.

Angela sat down. 'In that case it was a good job I came out to check on you. I was in the middle of a book, but it wasn't very interesting. There's no story that can match the intricacy of real life, is there?'

'None that I've read.'

Angela smiled. 'I don't know how long you've been lying there, but it's been an hour since I first noticed you. It's almost lunchtime, and since the rain sent us on our way yesterday, I thought we could try again today.' She nudged a picnic hamper sitting on the grass by her foot. It was like something out of an Enid Blyton story: a wicker frame and handle with the contents covered by a checkered blanket. 'I have pumpkin pie, camembert, apricot and ham sandwiches—which taste a lot better than they sound—and some chestnut pudding I rustled up this morning. All ingredients sourced from round here, or at my local organic supermarket. Oh, and coffee, in a very large flask.'

Jennifer smiled. 'Are you sure you're not some kind of fairy godmother?' she said. 'Because if you are, you've come along at exactly the right moment. Again.'

'Would that require me to wear some kind of fancy dress?' Angela asked, tilting her face so the sun caught it. 'It's a bit too chilly for that, I'm afraid. You're going to have to put up with jeans and a jacket.'

'It's better than nothing.'

Angela squatted down and pulled a picnic sheet out of

the bag. 'Much better to sit on this,' she said. 'You'll get a chill lying down like that.'

'Thanks.'

Jennifer sat up and repositioned herself on the blanket. Bonky had come back to life, and was busy dashing around them, chasing a late-season butterfly. A breeze rustled through the tree branches nearby, and the light chill of the wind seemed to welcome Jennifer back into the world.

'I think I lost it for a minute, there,' she said. 'I really don't know what's wrong with me.'

'Sometimes it's all right just to let the world pass by,' Angela said. 'None of us can stop it, after all. Just enjoy the passing moments. Be happy for what we have, and don't pine on what we don't. Look at me, I'm proper old and I still have hopes and dreams.'

'Like what?'

'Oh, nothing like changing the world, not at my age. Simple things, like seeing the children of my regulars playing in the fallen leaves this November. Seeing a blanket of snow over this hill right here come winter time.' Her eyes twinkled. 'Perhaps even meeting a nice toy boy to whisk me off to Paris. I've never been, you know.'

'Really?' Jennifer sighed. 'I've been twice. The first was on a school trip during Sixth Form, which I only remember because the bus broke down. The second was with Mark … only what I thought was going to be a romantic weekend turned out to be an excuse to meet a client. I only saw him for half an hour either side of the flights. I wandered around on my own.'

'At least you got to choose where to go.'

Jennifer smiled and looked up. 'That's true. It wasn't all that romantic, but there are some amazing chateaux and museums. I'll tell you what … half term's coming up. Why don't we go together, if you have nothing else on?'

Angela beamed. 'That would be fantastic.'

They sat in silence for a few minutes, watching a group of teenagers attempting to play with a frisbee while the wind picked up at the most inappropriate moments to throw the disc off course.

'Let's tuck in,' Angela said at last, then took to unloading the basket's contents on to the blanket. When the wonderful aromas attracted Bonky's attention, Angela pulled out a little plastic Tupperware pot. 'I even have something for you,' she said, holding out the pot's contents to the dog. 'A little dog food of my own invention.' Glancing at Jennifer, she said, 'You don't mind me feeding your dog?'

'Go ahead. Smells good enough for us to eat.'

'It's just a few mashed up leftovers,' Angela said. 'Perhaps I'll go into the gourmet dog food business.'

Bonky stuffed down his lunch in a few swift bites, then raced off to chase things. Angela turned to Jennifer.

'So, what happened?'

Jennifer told Angela about Mark, and what she had seen that morning. At the end, Angela just shrugged.

'But isn't that a good thing?' she said. 'He was already in your past, so now you can put it all to bed. He's moved on. I know you've been having second thoughts, but really, there's no need. The only reason you're looking back is because you're worried about looking forward. You're still young. You have your whole life ahead of you. No reason to be worrying about the past when the future's got so much going for it.'

Jennifer nodded. 'I know you're right. Of course I do. It's not so easy to switch feelings on and off, though, is it?'

Jennifer thought about Amy's obsession with Rick, even when he showed her no interest, and even appeared to have a woman on the go. She remembered all the times

Mark had left her frustrated by not showing up, ducking out early, talking through her, ignoring her, and how he had softened any anger she had tried to muster with his usual charming smile, and a promise that things would be better.

Well, they were now.

'That's the spirit.'

'What? I didn't do anything.'

'Yes, you did. You just growled under your breath. I heard it. You're giving him the mental cold shoulder, aren't you?'

'I'm trying.'

'Let's focus on the future. This pie is still slightly warm. Let's get into it before it's cold. Then we'll go down and take a wander across the courtyard, figure out where you're going to set up your stalls for the harvest festival.'

'Okay, sounds good. Any word from the council on Big Gerry?'

Angela laughed. 'Regina Clover was over there this morning with a tape measure, measuring the circumference of the trunk. She kept running out of length. Me and Tom had a right laugh.'

'You and Tom?'

'Yeah, didn't you bump into him? He was doing a little weeding over there first thing, but he had to go and pick up some supplies.'

'Oh.' Jennifer made a mental note to walk eastwards around the park rather than westwards next time.

'You sound crestfallen.'

'I'm really not.'

'Are you sure about that?'

'He's just a caretaker.'

Angela lifted an eyebrow. 'Is that what you think?'

'I didn't mean—'

'I imagine someone who cuts grass for a living is a step down from an investment banker, but are you sure one is better than the other?'

Jennifer blushed, feeling a little embarrassed by her assessment. 'I didn't mean it like that.'

Angela patted her on the arm. 'You'll figure it out one day,' she said. 'I was the same as you when I was younger. I grew up at the end of a lane on the edge of a forest, yet all I wanted to do was live in a big city and do all the things big city people do. By the time I was forty, all I wanted to do was live at the end of that lane again. Unfortunately, by the time I was forty, that lane no longer existed and neither did the forest. I had to settle for a happy medium, but on my days off I drive up to the woods and go mushroom picking or something else.' She chuckled. 'Wild swimming in freezing cold ponds, that kind of thing.'

'Seriously?'

Angela shrugged. 'You don't know happiness until you get out of five-degree water in the middle of January and wrap a warm blanket around you. Heavenly.'

'Can I come next time?'

'Sure.'

Jennifer sighed. 'I'm useless,' she said at last.

Angela laughed. 'No, you aren't. You're just young. It's a flaw we all go through, but it passes in time. By the time you reach sixty, you're pretty much the finished article.' She shrugged. 'A shame I'll never get there. Being fifty-nine forever has its downsides.'

Jennifer smiled. 'I bet.'

'Right, let's go figure out your festival plan,' Angela said. 'Just to the right of Big Gerry, that's where you'll get the most traffic. You want your class's stall to do the best, don't you?'

Jennifer laughed. 'Of course.'

16

ACTING AND OTHER DRAMAS

'PHEWFF,' Rick said, shaking his head as he took a sip from a Starbucks coffee Jennifer now knew he could only have bought by making a wide detour out of town to the nearest motorway services, 'That was some weekend. I almost called in sick this morning.'

'You got the shakes from too much of your grandmother's cocoa?' Jennifer said, flicking an eyebrow at him.

'Hit the clubs,' Rick said. 'Nearly tore me apart.'

Amy, who was using a toothpick to poke stuck bits of pencil lead out of a box of green and red pencil sharpeners, looked up and said, 'Where did you go?'

Rick shook his head and gave a smarmy grin as though he'd spent the weekend being dipped in honey by a troupe of burlesque dancers. 'Donald's on Friar Street,' he said. 'That new place. You'd never get in, Clair. You have to be over five feet.'

'I'm five foot one!' Amy said.

'Without standing on tiptoe.'

'Don't you mean McDonald's?' Jennifer said.

'A recluse like you would never know,' Rick said. 'But,

you know, I'm willing to lend you an education if you ever pull that pole out of your—'

At the front of the room, Greg Downton cracked a ruler against the teachers' noticeboard. 'Right, good to see you lot all showed up for work this morning,' he said. 'Well, apart from Colleen, who called in sick.' He rolled his eyes. 'I'll be covering the reception class today, god forbid.'

'Forbid!' Amy hissed at Rick. 'Maybe we can use that?'

'Tape over it, Clair,' Rick replied, rolling his eyes. Amy pouted, and began to attack her latest clogged pencil sharpener with feverish abandon.

'I hope all your classes are progressing well with your preparation for the harvest festival,' Downton said. 'It doesn't look like it's going to be cancelled, more's the pity. I got a memo from the council this morning that said they've stayed the execution on that dangerous old tree until at least the end of October.'

'Woo hoo!' Amy shouted, jumping out of her seat and knocking a box of pencils onto the floor.

'Calm down, Ms. Clairmont,' Downton said. 'Keep your activism at home, and preferably in a closet. The next thing I know you lot will want vegan school dinners. We're raising children, not cattle.'

'Wouldn't know it from some of mine,' Amy quipped under her breath to Jennifer, who gave her a reassuring smile.

'And then there's this horror circus of a teachers' drama,' Downton said. 'I trust everything is progressing smoothly?'

'We're all still alive,' Rick said. 'For now.'

'That's good news. I'd hate to be hiring new staff so close to the festival. Does anyone have anything they would like to add?'

Maud, sitting at a corner desk just for the meeting,

raised her hand. 'We're going over budget on the copier,' she said. 'Please keep your copies to black and white only.'

'And work related,' Downton added. 'Right, anyone else? No? Okay, get on with it.'

As teachers began to file out, Rick glanced at Jennifer and Amy, then took a last tug on his Starbucks. 'All right, off I go. Wish me luck with the devils. I'll need it.'

'Good luck!' Amy squawked, a little too loudly, gaining an awkward glance from Rick and a glare from Mrs Davis sitting on Amy's other side.

As Rick headed out, Jennifer leaned over his desk and took the plastic lid off his Starbucks coffee disposable cup.

'I knew it, she said, holding up a PG Tips teabag. He's trolling us.'

FOR ONCE, her class survived until lunch without any major dramas. While not yet feeling exactly comfortable, Jennifer definitely felt that she was starting to get the hang of managing them, and even though at times she still felt like the invisible woman Mark had created, other times—such as when she had to step in to prevent a fight over a tub of green poster paint between two boys—she felt more real than she had in a long time.

She was still a work in progress, but Angela's words echoed in her head.

As the bell rang for lunch and the kids put away their art supplies, Gavin Gordon approached the desk.

'Miss? Can I talk to you?'

'Sure.'

He waited until the rest of the kids had headed either to the dining hall or the playground before giving a little cough.

'Miss … I've decided who I want to be on my management team for the festival.'

'Yes?'

Gavin's cheeks reddened. 'First, Paul—'

'Paul Lemon? Is that wise?'

'He's strong. He can carry stuff.'

'Well, okay.'

'And you said there had to be at least one girl. So, uh, Kel and Bec.'

His cheeks were so red now Jennifer could have plucked them from a vine and put them up for sale in Tesco.

'Okay … have you asked them about this?'

'They said whatever.'

'Which means yes?'

Gavin shrugged. Jennifer figured she would just have to assume that a positive response had been returned unless told otherwise.

'And one more … because you said five. Uh … Matt.'

'Excuse me? You mean Matt Bridges?'

'Yeah.'

'The boy you've picked on since—by all accounts—the first year?'

Gavin's head shot up. 'I don't pick on him!'

'That's not what literally every child or teacher has ever told me, Gavin. If you're hoping this will give you a chance to bully him, I won't stand for it.'

Gavin gave a frantic shake of his head. 'No, it's not like that. It's … well, he has neat handwriting. He can do the price labels. And he's good at maths. He can do all the adding up and looking after the money.'

Jennifer smiled. 'I suppose that makes sense. Have you asked him yet?'

'Not yet. Maybe after lunch.'

'Well, you'd better hurry up about it. We don't have much time.'

'I know.'

As Gavin turned to head off for lunch, Jennifer cleared her throat. 'Ah, Gavin?'

'Yes, Miss?'

She smiled. 'Those are good choices. I think they'll make a good team.'

Gavin looked at the ground but didn't smile. 'Thanks, Miss.'

'How's your mum?'

Gavin shrugged. 'She's okay.'

'That's good. Go on, you'd better hurry up. You're missing playtime.'

'RIGHT, ARE WE READY?'

Amy, holding her script out in front of her like a priest about to begin a sermon, looked around the assembled group. Some shrugged, some grunted in agreement. Old Don sighed. Jennifer, standing to Amy's left, glanced at Rick, who was already making gestures in the air like a silent movie thespian, a look of total concentration on his face.

'Okay, final read through, then we'll do it with actions. Oh, I'm so excited!'

'Fire had engulfed the land,' Jennifer began, trying to sound dramatic in her role as part narrator, part minstrel. 'The war against the dragons had continued for all eternity. From the ashes of the country rose one man who could end the war forever. His name was … Sir Brent.'

Rick sniggered.

'Can you make it sound a little more … hopeless?' Amy said.

'I'm trying.'

'Lass's first time to act,' Colin Tiller said with a chuckle.

Jennifer cleared her throat. 'Fire had engulfed the land—'

'Try putting the stress on "engulfed",' Old Don Jones said. 'And hurry up about it. Lord Brent will have died of old age before he even gets out on his quest.'

'Sir Brent,' Collin Tiller said.

'Are you starting on me, you pompous old—'

'It's Sir Brent,' Rick said.

Amy gave a frantic clap of her hands. 'Let's start over again. From the top….'

AT SIX O'CLOCK, it came down to a vote whether to have one more run through, or call it a night. Amy enthusiastically voted yes, with Jennifer offering half an arm as moral support. The rest of the teachers were done, though, so time was called and they all headed home.

Jennifer, her throat aching from a day of shouting at the kids followed by practice of the newly inaugurated school song, and then drama practice, grabbed some take-away food on the way home, ate it on the sofa before mustering a last gasp of energy to take Bonky out for a walk.

It was a beautiful late September evening. Warm with a light breeze blowing through the trees, the sun leaving mottles of shadow across the paths. A few scatterings of leaves had already fallen, others were just beginning to change colour. Jennifer felt her stress draining away as she watched Bonky racing across the grass, vainly in pursuit of the pigeons hunting for seeds.

Angela was right. She had to look forward instead of back. Refusing to think about Mark or the past she had left behind, she tried to focus on the upcoming festival. It would surely pass without a hitch, but it surprised her how nervous she felt, particularly about the teachers' drama. It was hardly a showpiece, with the audience likely to be a handful of disinterested mums and dads and a few pupils hoping their teachers slipped up. Even so, she hadn't done any acting since school, and the thought of any audience whatsoever was terrifying.

She was just wondering whether it might be best to slug a quick glass of wine before going on, when she noticed a line of people heading into the theatre. She wandered over with Bonky and found that a new play had just opened, a local group performing a musical version of Shakespeare's Macbeth.

The evening show was due to start in half an hour. Not really giving herself time to think, Jennifer scooped Bonky up under her arm and jogged home, threw on some slightly more appropriate clothing and then dashed back to the theatre. As she headed in through the ticket gate, paid her five pounds for a stalls ticket, she hoped the server in the box office wouldn't notice the sweat beading along her brow. She made a quick toilet stop then found her seat, thankfully with a few spaces on either side of the sparsely populated theatre.

Like every British school kid who could actually read, she had absentmindedly studied some Shakespeare at school, but had largely forgotten it in the intervening years. Thankfully, this seemed to be a watered down and reworked version, as the first characters came out speaking in language that it was possible to understand, before breaking into song against a recorded background tape.

While not exactly the West End, Jennifer felt a little inspiration as she watched the way the characters walked around the stage, how they stood, how they gestured, and how they performed their lines. It was clearly an amateur group by the sparseness of the stage backs and costumes, but they performed with no little skill. She found herself nodding along to the first song, and had a smile on her face when a trumpet sound blew, and to a round of applause the main character came on stage.

He marched to the middle, spread his arms, and announced himself as Macbeth, future king of Scotland. Jennifer stared openmouthed. As the actor gave a cackling laugh for effect, she tried to shrink down in her seat, aware that all he had to do was look down to see her.

As the applause ended, his eyes scanned across the audience. Jennifer gave an embarrassed smile as Tom, dressed in a frilly shirt, black trousers and boots, with a toy sword hung at his hip, gave a double take as he spotted her, and nearly missed a step. Quickly hiding a look of surprise, he managed to recover his composure with professional grace and deliver his next line. As soon as another character took centre stage, he glanced back at Jennifer, flashed a smile and winked.

A couple of minutes later, he broke into a song. Jennifer watched in awe of Tom's stage presence, note perfect singing voice, and mastery of his lines. She quickly got over the shock of seeing him as an actor and found herself drawn into the story, a modified version of the original tragedy featuring a lot more humour, a scattering of borderline cheesy songs, and a couple of cool battle scenes.

And Tom, the gardener who raked leaves and caught injured ducks for a living, became something else entirely.

On stage he looked a natural, head and shoulders above the rest of the group, as though he had spent years working in theatre and knew all the tricks. Each time he took centre stage for a speech or a song, Jennifer found herself unable to look away.

At the end, instead of being murdered in the final battle, Macbeth dressed in drag and fled off into the night, intent on becoming a mummer in a travelling circus while biding his time to return to Scotland and take his revenge. The players lined up and took a bow to a standing ovation, Tom again flashing Jennifer a quick smile. Then the curtains came across, and the lights went up.

People began getting up and shuffling out. Only a couple of hundred spectators had been present to witness Tom's masterclass, but with daily showings for the next two weeks, Jennifer planned to return, perhaps with Angela or Amy. She waited for a couple of minutes, hoping Tom might come out, but the curtains stayed closed. Reluctantly, she headed for the exit.

Night had fallen during the performance, and Jennifer realised she had forgotten to bring any kind of jacket. Most of the other spectators were heading out of the doors and around to a car park in Sycamore Park's north-west corner, but she was faced with a slightly nervy walk along the tree-lined paths to the southern entrance. She was about to take her chances when a familiar voice hailed her.

She turned to see Tom striding across the lobby. He looked totally different from the man she knew as the park's caretaker, in black trousers and freshly polished shoes, his unkempt hair pressed beneath a thin-brimmed hat that was almost dapper. He wore a smart casual jacket and had a big grin on his face.

'Jennifer. Glad I caught you. Thanks for coming.'

She stared at him, unable to speak, giving just a brief nod of acknowledgement.

Tom spread his arms. 'What did you think? I fluffed a couple of lines, but it's an adapted version so I don't think anyone will have noticed.'

Jennifer swallowed. 'I didn't know you acted,' she said.

Tom smiled. 'It's only local. A bit of a hobby these days.'

'These days?'

He shrugged. 'I had a few small roles going back a while.'

'Small roles?'

'Some TV work. A bit of West End. I got tired of the industry, which is why I do what I do now.'

Jennifer started to say, 'A bit of West End?' but realised she was beginning to sound like a parrot so clamped her mouth shut. 'Oh,' was all she could bring herself to say. 'That's nice.'

Tom smiled, and Jennifer felt her starstruck heart melting. 'I didn't know you were into Shakespeare,' he said.

'Neither did I until now. I just came along to get some inspiration for the teachers' play.' She gave a nervous laugh. 'I'm a minstrel.'

'Well, if you like, I could stop by to one of your rehearsals sometime to give you a few tips. If you think anyone would be interested ... I don't want to intrude, but I'm happy to help.'

Jennifer nodded. 'I think that would be great. Amy wants us to put the Royal Shakespeare Company to shame, but I don't think we're going to pull that off. If we manage not to embarrass ourselves I'll be happy enough.'

Tom smiled. 'Sure. Just let me know a date and I'll check my schedule. First, let me drive you home. It's dark and getting chilly. I can't have you walking home.'

'Drive?'

'Yeah.' Tom lifted an eyebrow. 'I have a car, you know.'

'So you don't….'

His face shone with amusement. 'Live in that shack? Er, no. That's just a shed. I have a place across town. You didn't really think I lived there, did you?'

Jennifer gave a shy smile and shook her head, wondering how red it was possible to turn. She muttered an acceptance to the offer of a lift just to get away from the glaring lights in the theatre lobby as quickly as she possibly could.

Tom led her through the car park to a shiny Toyota that looked just a couple of years old. With another smile, Tom opened the passenger door for her, but it took Jennifer a couple of seconds to get her legs to move.

'Uh, thanks.'

'This is my car,' Tom said with a chuckle. 'I didn't steal it.'

'I know. I'm just struggling with this.'

'Being the park caretaker isn't my only job,' Tom said. 'In fact, it's more of a hobby than anything else. I like being out in the open air. I do a couple of other things that mostly involve sitting at a computer. Some voiceover work, stuff like that. Just to pay the rent.'

Jennifer got into the car. Tom climbed in and they set off. A couple of minutes later, they pulled up outside Jennifer's building on Willis Lane.

'Ah, thanks,' Jennifer said, opening the door. Still feeling starstruck, she said, 'I'd, uh, invite you up but you know, the cat and the dog might get jealous.'

Tom laughed. 'And this is a double yellow. Thanks again for coming to the show, Jennifer. It made my night seeing you in the audience. See you around?'

She nodded. 'For sure.'

A light patter of rain had begun to fall. Jennifer climbed out, shut the door, and retreated to her building's porch, from where she waved to Tom and watched him drive away. As his rear brake lights flashed and then he turned out of sight, she tried to suppress the butterflies making a stage musical of their own in her stomach.

17

DASHED DREAMS

'YOU DIDN'T TELL me Tom was an actor,' Jennifer said to Angela, trying not to sound too admonishing.

Angela chuckled around a mouthful of quiche. She patted her lips with a handkerchief and shook her head. 'Is he?'

'You know he is.'

'Well, I knew he dabbled.'

'He does a lot more than dabble. I looked him up on the internet. He's been in tons of stuff. He's practically Brentwell's most famous son. I'm surprised he hasn't been given the keys to the city or whatever.'

'It doesn't have any gates.'

'Well, if it did….'

Angela continued to chuckle. 'Does it make a difference? About whether you like him or not?'

'That he's been in something like thirty TV shows, and spent three years playing the second lead in Les Misérables in the West End? Of course it does.'

'Ah, but he's technically retired. He told me he only joined the cast of Macbeth: Revisited for something to do during the evenings. He's not on TV anymore.'

'So you do know that he's an actor?'

Angela just shrugged. 'It might have come up in conversation from time to time. I never really felt it relevant to mention.'

'I'm not on a job interview!'

'Calm down. Following the same principles, I've not, for example, told Tom that you abandoned your ex while he was away on a golfing weekend in order to make a new life for yourself here in Brentwell. I didn't feel that was relevant. I did mention that you always pick the hazelnuts out of pies and that you get a little talkative after the third glass of wine. Such things I felt of high relevance, should you two ever make it as far as a date.'

Jennifer grimaced. 'Point taken. Wait a minute. Date? Are you trying to set me up?'

'Oh, no. I really don't have the energy for that. I'm merely offering you a little guidance here and there, attempting to steer you in the right direction, so to speak.'

'I'm not interested in Tom.'

'I thought you just said you were.'

'I meant … as a person. He pretends to be a park caretaker but he's actually one of Britain's most respected method actors, just hiding out here in Sycamore Park.'

'Oh, he's not hiding. He gets paid. He works for the council.'

'Well, you know what I mean.'

Angela patted Jennifer on the arm. 'Look, calm down a little and have some more wine. There's plenty of time to worry about all these things. You're still young. Oh, and talking of which, it's my birthday on Friday. Do you think you could suffer an old woman for a quiet night on the town? I haven't been out anywhere in years.'

Jennifer grinned. 'Of course. Do you want to make a proper party of it?'

'Oh no, just a couple of drinks, perhaps a little dance. I was quite a mover in my youth, don't you know. However, these days, turning … fifty-nine, I don't have quite the flexibility I once had. More's the pity.'

'I'd be delighted to chaperone you for the night,' Jennifer said. 'I've not really been out anywhere since I got here. As long as we don't go to Donald's on Friar Street, in case my sleazy colleague is there.'

'Donald's? Don't you mean McDonald's?'

Jennifer shrugged. 'Maybe it has a party room?'

'Perhaps we could invite Tom to chaperone both of us,' Angela said. 'Although I'd hate to be a gooseberry.'

'Let's just make it a girls' night,' Jennifer said.

Angela clapped her hands together. 'Fantastic. We'll get really drunk and discuss your love life. Another glass of wine?'

JAMES WAS SLEEPING on her pillow with Bonky positioned midway along the bed when Jennifer got home, as though to suggest that she was neglecting them somewhat. She took Bonky for a quick walk down to the corner of Sycamore Place, although it was too dark to venture into the park. Bonky seemed content to inspect the line of bushes along the roadside, but Jennifer looked up at the park's entrance, illuminated by streetlights, with a sense of longing. Only now as she thought about it, did she realise how the patch of trees, paths, ponds, and rock features had become so central to the rebooted edition of her life, like a central cog around which she could begin to revolve. For the first time in several days she had thought more about what she had gained than what she had left behind.

And it felt good.

Bonky wandered on a few steps, tugging on his lead. Jennifer followed, staring absently at a leaflet taped to a nearby bus shelter while the dog nosed in the bushes nearby.

Proposal for Change of Land Use:
Sycamore Park Northwest Corner

Meeting open to the public
Saturday 2nd October
Brentwell Town Hall – North Building 2nd Floor Rm 12
Hosted by Councillor Regina Clover

Below the heading were a few paragraphs outlining the proposal. The entire northwest corner, encompassing Big Gerry and his surrounds, was considered an ideal location for a new water treatment plant to reduce the load on the current treatment plant to the north of the city.

Jennifer stared. A sewage works. Right on the edge of Sycamore Park. The view from Angela's café would be devastated, the beautiful trees replaced by barbed wire fences, tanker lorries, and KEEP OUT signs, the gentle breeze through the tree branches replaced by the hum of generators and the tinkle of sprinkler systems.

Regina Clover, she of the beautiful name but blackened heart, was the host. Jennifer pulled out her phone and took a photo of the notice. She would be there, and she hoped other local residents from the park's vicinity would be too.

This could not be allowed to happen. No sooner had

Jennifer found a sense of peace, then it was about to be derailed.

'Come on, Bonky,' Jennifer said, tugging his lead as a chill wind rushed down Sycamore Place as though to remind Jennifer of the impending doom, 'We have work to do.'

18

TRAFFIC LIGHTS

'Miss, we've got three mums making cheesecake,' Gavin said, frowning as he held out his scribbled handwritten list. 'We can't have three cheesecakes.'

Jennifer put down the pen she was using to mark that morning's maths test and looked up at Gavin.

'What do you think we should do?'

Gavin's jaw hardened. 'If I thump Steve Thomas maybe he'll tell his mum to make fruitcake instead.'

Jennifer winced. 'I don't think that will help.'

'It was a joke, Miss.'

'Well, what else can we do?'

Gavin's lower lip trembled. The last thing Jennifer wanted to do was make the boy cry, but if she was ever going to instil confidence into him, she had to encourage him to solve problems for himself.

'I don't know, Miss.'

'What kind of cheesecake do you like, Gavin?'

His expression changed to one of pure pleasure. 'Strawberry. Mum gets this one off the deli counter in Tesco. It's great.'

'What kind don't you like?'

Gavin's nose wrinkled. 'Banana. It's rank. It tastes like a dog's—'

'Sure, I get it,' Jennifer said, putting up a hand. 'But some people might like it, otherwise they wouldn't sell it, would they?'

'Yeah, but they're dickheads.'

Jennifer winced again. 'But even so—'

Gavin's eyebrows lifted. 'So what you reckon is, we could get them to make different kinds of cheesecake?'

Jennifer clenched a fist under the table. 'That's a great idea, Gavin. You could ask them to make different kinds, so that even the dickheads have something they can eat.'

'Miss, you can't say dickhead.'

Jennifer smiled. 'I won't tell anyone you said it, if you do the same for me. Secret?'

Gavin gave a frantic nod. 'Okay. You're all right, Miss. Better than Old Goldsmith.'

The sense of satisfaction Jennifer felt had a guilty veneer, kind of like eating too much low fat chocolate.

'Why, thank you, Gavin. It's nice of you to say so. By the way, how are things at home?'

Gavin beamed again. 'Dad's taking me to the game on Saturday,' he said.

'Is that right? Who are you going to see?'

'Argyle.'

'Oh, that's too bad.'

Gavin appeared to ignore her. 'Dad's signed us up for the supporter's club. We can go to all the home games for free, and get discounts on away. We've got new season kits and everything. I reckon we're going to win the league this year.'

'Are Argyle in a league?'

'Two. Means we only need to win promotion three times in a row to be in the Premiership.'

'Well, good luck.' She smiled. 'I'm glad things are going well. Anyway, you'd better get off to lunch.'

As Gavin raced off after the other kids, Jennifer let out a sigh of relief. So far, so good. The council building was not far from the town museum, so after attending the proposal meeting at the town hall, she would stop in and see Marlie, let her know that Gavin seemed happy. Parents' evening was next Wednesday, but Gavin's mother might not be able to attend.

Jennifer glanced at her watch. She was on playground duty today, but if she was quick, she could still run back to the staffroom for a quick coffee. With Angela's birthday bash tonight, she needed all the caffeine she could get.

ANGELA, wearing a beige blouse so bright it was almost yellow under a fake fur jacket which made her look more like an elegant Duchess than a café owner, frowned at Jennifer and shook her head.

'No, that will never do. You can't wear dark blue on my birthday. Wait here a second.'

She went into the café's kitchen. Jennifer heard another door open and close. She waited, shifting from foot to foot, then sipped from a glass of wine Angela had given her. She looked at the book on Zen living and the pot plant Angela had recently unwrapped, hoping her new friend liked her hastily bought presents.

'Here we are,' Angela said, coming back in. She held up a pretty one-piece. 'This should be about your size.'

'It's ... uh, yellow.'

'Amber, dear. Not yellow.'

'Why do I have to wear yellow?'

'Amber. It's my favourite colour, and it's my choice, so there.'

'But—'

'It's my birthday.'

Jennifer suppressed a groan. 'Sure. If that's what you want, I'll wear it.'

No sooner had she changed into the dress and stood frowning at herself in a wall mirror beside the café's kitchen, than a knock came on the door.

'Come in!' Angela called.

The door opened. Tom's face appeared. He wore a sheepish grin, and a lemon yellow shirt that was so ghastly it made Jennifer feel better about her own dress, even if she was struggling to overcome the shock of Tom's appearance.

'Ah, Tom, there you are,' Angela said.

'Sorry I'm a bit late,' Tom said.

'Why's he coming?' Jennifer whispered to Angela as Tom turned to hang a jacket up on a hook beside the door. 'I thought it was just us. Are you trying to set me up?'

'We need some muscle in case we get into a fight,' Angela said with a mischievous grin. 'And someone to carry us home if we get too drunk.'

Jennifer grimaced. 'Hi, Tom,' she said. 'You look … nice.'

'I managed to find this monstrosity in Oxfam,' Tom said. 'Is it yellow enough for you, Angela?'

'That will do nicely. My birthday, everyone wearing my favourite colour. Perfect.' She clapped her hands together. 'Shall we get going, or do you want to slam some tequilas first?'

'Ah, let's just get going,' Jennifer said, glancing around the interior of the café, wondering why, if yellow was

Angela's favourite colour, there was little evidence of it among all the oranges and browns.

Angela wanted to walk, so they headed in the direction of Brentwell's little centre, stopping at a couple of pubs on the way, so they could "warm up", as Angela liked to put it. Angela, laughing and joking, was the light and soul of everything, but as the drinks began to flow, Jennifer found herself talking with greater freedom to Tom.

'I remember laughing at the school caretaker when I was at school,' Tom said. 'Here's this old guy and all he does is cut the grass or trim the hedges. He comes to school in a beat up old Ford, and his clothes could have come from any of the charity shops. We used to call him Worzel Gummidge behind his back. And then I get older, and I realise that sitting behind a desk all day, dressed in a suit I'm scared to scuff or spill coffee on, warmed by a heater, cooled by an air-conditioner, having someone ball me out because I forgot to press a number on a computer screen … I finally got it. That guy, that caretaker, he understood what life was really about.'

'I'm sorry,' Jennifer said. 'I really did think you were a bumpkin. I'm so shallow.'

'You're not shallow at all,' Tom said. 'In fact, there are few people I've ever met who have so much going on, so many layers—'

'Time to move on, you two!' Angela called. 'Are you ready for the main event?'

Jennifer glanced at Tom, who shrugged.

'Where next?' Jennifer said.

'Gossip Bar,' Angela said.

Tom stared. 'Seriously? The old person's place?'

Angela laughed and patted Jennifer on the shoulder. 'Did you bring your ID?'

'What for? I'm thirty-six.'

'But you look much younger. They might refuse you entry.'

'Why?'

Tom cringed. 'Gossip Bar is over-thirties only. You're not allowed in otherwise.'

'Sounds great. I won't have to look at all the bright young things and be reminded of my long-ago youth.'

'You think yours was long ago?' Angela said. 'Queen Victoria was on the throne when I was young. I bet I'll still be first on the dancefloor, though.'

'Is that a challenge?'

'You bet it is.'

'Then let's go.'

THE SKY WAS CLOUDING OVER, the sun about to set as they headed up the high street. A line of people stood outside Gossip Bar, waiting under an awning to gain entry. Jennifer stared. Except for one older couple who looked equally bemused, everyone standing in the queue wore either red, green or yellow. Jennifer glanced at Tom, who shrugged, then at Angela, who wore another impish smile.

'Ah, what's going on?' Jennifer asked.

'Oh, nothing much,' Angela said. 'It's just traffic light night, that's all.'

'Uh, what?'

Tom was chuckling. 'Oh my, I haven't been to one of these in twenty years. So, that explains this god-awful set up you've got us wearing.'

'It'll be fun,' Angela said.

'Um, I've lived under a rock my whole life,' Jennifer said. 'Enlighten me, please.'

'It's a pick up night,' Tom said. 'Red means you're

taken, green that you're available. Yellow means that you're a maybe.'

'A maybe?'

Tom nodded. 'Potentially in a relationship, but willing to be swayed if the right person comes along.'

'You have to wear yellow, otherwise you get swamped,' Angela said.

Jennifer frowned. 'Are you a regular at these things?'

Angela laughed. 'Oh, not for a while. I was quite the raver in my youth, though.'

They joined the back of the queue as people filed inside. As they reached the entrance, the doorman stuck out a hand. 'I.D.?'

Jennifer smiled. 'Oh, wait—'

'I mean her.' The doorman frowned at Angela.

'Oh, Gary, you're such a tease.'

The doorman burst into laughter. 'Come on in, folks. Oh, hey Tom. You're on escort duty tonight?'

'Escorting these two ladies home only,' Tom said.

'Well, have a good one.'

'Thanks, mate.'

They headed into the club. A dancefloor in one corner was filled with people, the music a little quieter than Jennifer remembered from her last venture into a club, perhaps to appease the older audience. They got drinks from a bar and found a table in a corner.

'Well, happy birthday,' Jennifer said to Angela, and the three of them clinked glasses.

'I think I might go and have a dance,' Angela said, jumping up and heading for the dancefloor before the others could react.

'She's quite the livewire,' Jennifer said to Tom. 'I don't know how she keeps it up.'

'It's all that healthy living,' he said. 'We should probably take a leaf out of her book.'

'So I'll see you in the park for yoga at sunrise?'

'I'll be there with my leotard on,' Tom said.

Jennifer was about to respond when she noticed someone wearing a bright green t-shirt moving through the crowd in her direction.

'Oh my god, hide me,' she said, leaning behind Tom.

'What?'

'That guy over there, he's from my school.'

'In the green t-shirt? He's a bit young to be in here, isn't he?'

'Yeah, that's him. Don't let him see me, please.'

Rick, cocksure and full of swagger, moved through the crowd with a smug pout on his face. As he got closer, Jennifer peeked out from behind Tom's shoulder to see that Rick's t-shirt was actually threaded with green fairy lights that flickered as he walked. She ducked out of sight as he got closer, and for a moment thought he had seen her. Then, glancing up, she saw he had stopped at the next table, where two attractive women in their mid-thirties were chatting over glasses of wine.

'Excuse me, ladies,' Rick said. 'The hue of your attire suggests you could be swayed. I'd like to make a suggestion.'

'Is this guy for real?' Tom whispered to Jennifer, who was still cowering behind him. He wore an amused smirk as he watched Rick's move on the women.

'Just don't let him see me,' Jennifer hissed.

'So, the sad fact is this,' Rick said, looking from one of the women to the other, as they both gazed up at him like mothers watching a child performing in a school play. 'And I'm pretty sure you'll feel for me when I say this … but I can't really choose between you. I'm equally bewitched. In order to solve this problem, I think you should play rock, paper, scissors. The winner gets to come home with me, while the loser unfortunately will have to wait for another time. In the unfortunate event that it's a draw, I guess I'll just have to take you both home.'

The two women laughed. Jennifer cringed, for a moment fearing they had been taken in by Rick's schoolboy charm. Then one of them shook her head and said, 'I'm sorry, but I have RSI.'

'You have what?'

'RSI.'

'What's that?'

'Repetitive strain injury. It puts me at an unfair advantage, and I'd hate to miss out on such an opportunity purely by default.'

'How'd you end up with that?'

'I'm a secretary. I work for the school board, typing up school reports. How many A grades did you get?'

'What … I—'

The other cupped a hand around her ear. 'Isn't that your mother calling?'

Rick spun around, looking towards the dancefloor. 'What? Where?'

The two women closed ranks, moving to face each other, and Rick, after a brief pout in their direction, headed off to try his luck elsewhere.

'Wow, that was close,' Jennifer said. 'That's Rick. He sits next to me at work, more's the pity. Fancies himself as a ladykiller. I hope Angela keeps her head down. Looks like she's getting some attention.'

Jennifer stared. Halfway across the dancefloor, Angela was bopping and jiving to some obscure eighties disco track. Close by, an older man was doing a pretty good frogin-a-blender impression. Every time he caught Angela's gaze, she burst out laughing.

'It gets worse,' Jennifer said. 'Are there any sinkholes around here I can jump into?'

'You don't know that guy, do you?'

Jennifer cringed and nodded. 'Yeah, I do. He's the headmaster of Brentwell Primary, Greg Downton. My boss.'

19

HEDGEHOGS AND CHILLI SAUCE

Jennifer woke up with a start. She rolled over, receiving a whine from Bonky and a lazy miaow from James as she shifted the pair off her legs. She rubbed her head, for a moment all sorts of crazy thoughts going through her mind as she tried to recall last night's events.

She had definitely drunk too much. More than she had in years. Had she pulled Tom? No. It had been extremely tempting, but she could clearly remember him waving goodbye as he walked back up Willis Lane, having walked both Angela and herself home. Had Angela pulled Greg Downton? She was less certain about that. She definitely hadn't been seen by Rick, but Greg had given her a long hard stare at one point, as though looking at a mirage. With a little luck, he would have forgotten by Monday.

Bonky was whining to go out. Throwing on some clothes, Jennifer grabbed the little dog's lead and headed for Sycamore Park.

It was a beautiful October morning. The sun shone through trees beginning to turn orange and red. Letting Bonky nose around the bushes, Jennifer bought a coffee and a breakfast roll from Pete's van and sat on a bench to let her hangover clear. After a few minutes of the chilly breeze ghosting her face, she began to smile. A little spider was spinning a web on a corner of the bench, and she gave one of the new threads a gentle nudge. The spider, disturbed, raced back to the bench, taking up residence on her knee for a couple of minutes before resuming its activities.

A month after moving to Brentwell, she felt like she was finally beginning to spin her own web. She had new friends, she had ambitions, and she was quickly building up a series of memories that kept a smile on her face. When she looked back on her time with Mark she found it hard to smile at all: so many times he would come home on a Friday and announce he was leaving early on Saturday for a golfing or some other team building event. Then there were voicemails left on their house phone which felt like a foreign language, congratulating Mark on some achievement he'd never even mentioned, or inviting him to yet another event. There was the time he came home with a brand new Lexus, the how and why he had purchased such a thing a mystery to Jennifer as she continued to slowly fade away into invisibility.

'I am me,' she said out loud. 'I am Jennifer Stevens of Willis Lane, Brentwell, a school teacher at Brentwell Primary.'

'Wow, how drunk did you get yesterday?' came a voice from behind her, and Jennifer nearly fell off the bench as she jumped up and spun around. What was left of her coffee splashed across the grass, and she had to make an awkward grab for her breakfast roll wrapper as the breeze threatened to send it cartwheeling down the path.

Tom, wearing his caretaker's overalls, was crawling on the ground behind a line of nearby bushes.

'Oh, sorry about that,' he said, standing up. 'I didn't mean to startle you.'

Jennifer picked up her litter and brushed herself down to regain her composure. 'Are you spying on me?'

Tom laughed. 'Absolutely not. Come and have a look at this little chap.'

Jennifer squatted down beside Tom, who had lifted up a branch of the nearest bush and was peering underneath.

'See him?'

'Oh. That's a … hedgehog?'

The little ball of needles shifted a little. 'I scared him,' Tom said. 'He should be finding somewhere to nest for the winter by now, but it looks like he's a little late. Luckily I have some hedgehog houses around the back of the shack over there.'

'Some what?'

'I'll show you.'

He reached into his pocket and pulled out a pair of thick gardening gloves. As he did so, Bonky came wandering over.

'Quick, don't let him get too close,' Tom said. He pulled on the gardening gloves and scooped up the little hedgehog while Jennifer put Bonky back on his lead. 'Right, this way,' Tom said.

Around the back of the shack were a line of what looked like rabbit hutches but lower to the ground and without any way to see inside. A small opening allowed access, and Tom lifted up the top of the nearest one to reveal a bundle of straw.

'They can go in and out as they please,' he said. 'The tunnel is too narrow for foxes or badgers to get in, so they're safe. We'll just put him in here for a bit and let him nose around to see if he likes it. Once he's got his smell in there, he might decide to come back.'

He put the little hedgehog down in the straw. It immediately uncurled and began to nose around. Tom smiled as he lowered the lid.

'Right, I think I owe you a coffee,' he said. 'Plus, I haven't eaten yet this morning. Can I interest you in seconds?'

Jennifer smiled. 'Sounds great. Uh … I was just wondering … I didn't pull you last night, did I?'

Tom laughed. 'I'm afraid I'm not in the business of taking advantage of drunken women. I made sure both you and Angela got safely into your houses, alone and with both your possessions and integrity intact. However, I was flattered by the attempts.'

'Attempts … plural?'

Tom laughed again. 'You got very affectionate after your fifth or sixth tequila. I'm surprised you're looking so fresh today.'

Jennifer, glad the chill wind was hiding her blush, shrugged. 'I suppose I must still be young.'

'That kebab you nailed outside Gossip Bar would have soaked most of it up.'

'Kebab?'

'You don't remember? You and Angela had a race. She lost because she'd doubled down on the chili sauce. I imagine she's feeling a little sore this morning.'

Jennifer cringed. 'Was I embarrassing?'

'Not at all. I found you rather … charming.' Before Jennifer could respond, he started off in the direction of Pete's van. 'Come on. Let's get those coffees in before this gets awkward.'

Jennifer trailed Tom towards Pete's van, Tom regularly checking over his shoulder to see if she was following. Had she really tried to pull him? Perhaps it was time to ease up on the drink a little.

Tom was already engaged in conversation when she reached the van. 'I found this in the weeds,' Tom said, handing Pete what looked like the corner of a bathroom tile. 'Not sure if you can use it….'

'Is that red? Yeah, if you find any more, save them for me.'

'Will do. Two coffees, please.'

'Coming up.'

'What was that about?' Jennifer asked, as they walked back in the direction of Tom's shack.

'What?'

'That thing with the bit of tile.'

'Oh, that? Pete's an artist in his spare time. He makes mosaics. Hasn't he mentioned it? He had an exhibition last year up at the library.'

Jennifer shook her head. 'I had no idea.'

Tom laughed. 'Even in a place like this, you'd be amazed what you can find under the surface.'

'Does everyone around here have a secret life?'

'It's not a secret. I don't hide that I used to be on television. I just don't make a big song and dance about it.' He grinned. 'Not unless you ask, or you ply me with too much alcohol.'

'Is that why you took it easy last night? Were you at risk of turning John Travolta on the dance floor?'

'I was about one beer short.'

'I'll have to remember that for next time.'

Jennifer glanced at Tom and found him looking at her with a smile on his face. She looked quickly away, and he laughed.

'So, what have you got on today?' he said.

'I'm going to that meeting with Regina Clover,' she said. 'About the proposed water treatment plant.'

Tom's smile dropped. 'Oh, that. I have to work today,

otherwise I'd be tempted to go. Not sure I could handle it without throwing a few chairs, though. Don't worry, there's absolutely no way they'll pass that motion.'

'Are you sure?'

Tom sighed. 'I hope I am,' he said.

20

MEMORIES AND MEETINGS

AFTER SAYING GOODBYE TO TOM, Jennifer took Bonky back home, spent an hour watching TV while petting James, then gave her flat a quick clean before heading back out. She went over to the café to see if Angela wanted to come, but Angela, looking a little worse for wear, was busy with a large party of elderly people who had stopped by to take pictures of the changing leaves.

'I'll give her hell for you,' Jennifer said. 'By the way, you didn't pull my school's headmaster, did you?'

Angela laughed, then rubbed her head. 'What happens on the dance floor stays on the dance floor,' she said, giving Jennifer a wink. 'Although if you bury Regina quickly enough and come back to help me out, I might spill my secrets.'

'I'll see what I can do.'

A couple of dozen people had gathered for the proposal meeting. Regina, looking sinister in a sharp black dress suit, gave an hour long PowerPoint presentation so dull a couple of elderly people in front of Jennifer actually started to snore. She droned on and on about decontamination tanks and water flow indicators and all manner of other jargon that left Jennifer wishing she'd paid a little more attention during geography class. They were forty-five minutes in before Sycamore Park was even mentioned, and then Regina spun the angle that Big Gerry's corner was unsafe, unused, and unimportant, tapping her palm as she repeated the Three U's mantra.

By the time she had finished, Jennifer was so bored she was practically ready to offer the school field if Regina would just shut up. When Regina said, 'Any questions?' she joined her hand to a couple of others that lifted with tired disinterest.

'Will you replace the lost area of parkland with a new park elsewhere?' asked an old man in the front row.

'Studies have shown that park usage has declined sharply in the last decade,' Regina said. 'Such land could be put to better uses.'

'Okay….'

Another hand went up. 'Don't you like trees?'

'On the contrary, I have several in my garden,' Regina said, a thin smile on her lips, then lifted her pointy, spear-like arm in Jennifer's direction.

'I'm a teacher at the local school,' Jennifer said. 'Some of those trees are hundreds of years old. You're not just planning to destroy part of the park, but part of the town's history. How do you feel about that?'

'You can't keep everything, just because it's old,' Regina said. 'Otherwise we'd all be living in mud huts and driving Robin Reliants.'

A couple of people actually laughed at Regina's pitiful attempt at a joke. Jennifer, still numb from the presentation, couldn't find the will to argue.

'So, are we done here?' Regina said, looking around.

Jennifer wanted to argue more, but a shuffling of chairs

announced that the rest of the audience was keen to leave. She dutifully stood up and followed the others out, feeling like she had just got out of an overlong detention.

'THERE'S no way they'll pass it,' Angela said, putting a bowl of stew down in front of Jennifer. 'They can't. They just can't. When I saw one of those posters, I thought it was a joke. Cutting down Big Gerry is bad enough, but to turn the whole area into a water treatment plant … impossible. The woman's gone mad.'

'What would you do?' Jennifer asked.

Angela shrugged. 'Change the café's name to the Treatment Plant View Café?' She shrugged. 'I don't know. It would ruin me. Who wants to sit and look at something like that? It doesn't matter how good the food is. I suppose I could turn into a takeaway, but people don't tend to order stews and salads for takeaway, do they?' She shook her head. 'We'll have to just hope the council doesn't pass the motion.'

'I'll send out another letter at school tomorrow,' Jennifer said. 'And I'll set up an online petition and ask the children's parents to sign it. We can't give this up without a fight.'

'You'll get in trouble again,' Angela said. 'Didn't Greg give you a warning?'

Jennifer lifted an eyebrow. 'Um, Greg? Are we on first name terms with my school headmaster now?'

Angela chuckled, then shrugged. 'Oh, he stopped by this morning for breakfast. A very pleasant man. I don't know why you don't like him.'

Jennifer grimaced. 'It's not a case of not liking him, it's that he's my boss and I have to revile him by default.'

'Well, perhaps you should give him a bit of leeway. Oh, and he said his favourite so far is Louis.'

'Louis? What are you talking about?'

'It seems there's a snitch in your staffroom keeping him up to date with all the latest nicknames. He likes Louis the best. As in Louis Pasteur. Pastor? He thought that one was pretty inventive.'

Jennifer chuckled. 'That was one of Amy's. She'll be delighted but terrified at the same time.'

'I don't think he knows who's making them up. I got the impression he was rather flattered that someone would bother.'

'So, are you two like … an item?'

Angela gave another delightful chuckle. 'Oh, dear, I'm far too busy for a toy boy.' Then she leaned forward and giggled, almost childlike. 'But, you know … I won't be fifty-nine forever.'

'You will.'

'Oh, I certainly hope so.'

AFTER DINNER, Jennifer refused Angela's offer to open another bottle of wine, instead deciding to head home through Sycamore Park before it got too dark. The evenings were beginning to draw in, but with the clocks not going back until the end of the month, there were still a few weeks of late sunsets left to enjoy. Instead of cutting across the grassy knoll in the park's centre, she took the circular path heading east through Big Gerry's courtyard, where she paused for a while, gazing up at the giant tree's branches. How much change had such a tree seen? Cars would have been but a pipedream when the first seedling had appeared out of the ground, and if left alone, Big

Gerry would still be leaning over this courtyard long after Jennifer's time was over. It was ridiculous to think the council wanted to cut the tree down, and even worse that Regina Clover wanted to replace the entire area with a water treatment plant.

A handful of hardy mothers were watching their kids still running around in the playground, even as the wind got up, sending showers of leaves across the play apparatus, and the sun dipped towards the horizon. Jennifer waved hello to a couple she recognised whose older children went to her school, then said good evening to Pete, who was packing up his stall for the night.

As she walked back towards her flat, she felt a warm knot in her stomach, despite the wind, and certainly not to do with Angela's fine choice of wine. Mark, whether willingly or not, had stripped her of an identity, a place in the world, yet here, in this leafy little corner of Brentwell she was starting to find it again.

And she couldn't let Regina Clover and her County Council minions take it away.

As she walked past the lamp post on Willis Lane where she had seen the posting for the proposed meeting, she found it still taped, but one corner fluttering in the wind. In frustration she ripped it off before panicking about littering and making sure to fold it and stuff it deep into her jacket pocket.

Then she headed for home.

21

CRUTCHES AND CAKES

'I HEARD the staff party went off,' Amy said, managing to look both thrilled and heartbroken at the same time. 'I was gutted that I had to leave early, but I'd forgotten about my hair appointment.' She touched the lower edge of a bob that looked little different to last week. 'How does it look?'

'Like you're a different person. I almost thought Amy had quit and been replaced.'

Amy tittered. 'Oh, you're too kind. Do you think Rick will notice?'

'I'm certain he will, although he might not say anything, being shy and all that.'

'You really think he's shy?'

Jennifer spread her hands. 'Well, you know what they say, the shyest types are usually the loudest in the room.'

'Do they say that?'

'Yeah … so the party? I mean, I had plans and everything—'

'I'm so sorry I didn't call you. I mean, I think it was supposed to be a boys' night, but I forgot my keys and just kind of came back into the room at the right time, just as they were planning which pubs to hit up. I heard they went to Gossip Bar … have you ever been there?'

Taking the chance that no one had seen her, Jennifer shook her head. 'No, never.'

Amy leaned closer. 'It was traffic light night,' she hissed. 'Do you think Rick pulled?'

'I'm pretty sure he didn't.'

'What if he did? What if that's why he's late? Because he's been in the sack all weekend and he's worn out? What if….' Amy's eyes had glassed over. Jennifer looked around, scoping out the nearest box of tissues just in case. She was about to grab one off the desk opposite, when the staffroom door banged open. A metal pole with a plastic pad on the end poked inside, holding the door, then Rick stumbled in, crutches under each arm. He paused to glare around the room as though defying anyone to speak, then hobbled over to his desk and sat down.

For a few seconds no one spoke. Rick poked at a pile of marking beside his computer, then opened his desk drawer and dropped his phone inside. Then, looking up at Jennifer and Amy, he said, 'I suppose you're wondering who jumped me and how many I took down before they got the best of me?'

Jennifer grimaced. 'Something like that.'

'I'm guessing at least six,' Amy said.

'It was a hit and run,' Rick said. 'Friday night. I was chasing this girl across the street. Well, not chasing, but just kind of continuing a conversation. She was wearing red. This guy swerved and went straight into me.'

'Oh my, are you all right?'

'I'm fine, Clair. Considering. I must have gone thirty feet through the air. He slapped the cast on his leg. It's just a sprain, but the doctor wanted to play it safe. I could have walked out of there, but you know what the NHS is like, overprotective and all that.'

'Are you going to press charges?'

'It was just some grandma,' Rick said with a shrug. 'I couldn't put her through that. She'd probably have a heart attack.'

'You're a saint,' Jennifer said. 'But I thought you said it was a hit and run?'

'Isn't that what they call it?'

'Not if they don't run.'

Rick rolled his eyes. 'You're such a stickler for details. Where were you Friday night, anyway? At home painting your dog's nails?'

Jennifer smiled. 'Grooming the cat,' she said. 'Such an arduous task. So you went to Gossip Bar, I hear? Isn't that an oldies club?'

Rick shrugged. 'I'm a bit of a man for charity.'

'I thought you were twenty-eight? How did you get in?'

Rick just rolled his eyes. 'I must look older.'

'You look about seventeen, except on Monday mornings.'

'Thanks, I think.'

'He got IDed,' came a chortling laugh from a couple of desks over. Old Don stood up and swiped his comb-over back across his scalp. 'He had some fake thing he'd made. Didn't you, Rick?'

Rick just scowled. 'Well, while you lot stand around gasbagging, I'd better get going to class. I could have taken a week off sick, but I'm too dedicated to my job.'

Jennifer grinned. 'I'm sure your class appreciates it.'

'Do you want a dead arm?'

'Gavin!'

Jennifer leapt out from behind her desk with the awkwardness of a drunken triple-jumper, getting past a desk piled with boxes of old crayons and between Gavin and Matthew before Gavin's raised fist could carry out any action. She steered him away, pointing to the corridor.

'Out there. Now. Wait for me.'

As Gavin marched off, head lowered, Jennifer turned to Matthew. The little boy's bottom lip was trembling, but he was yet to burst into tears.

'Are you all right?'

Matthew gave a solemn nod. Jennifer looked at him for a few more seconds as other kids crowded around, then gave him a reassuring pat on the shoulder.

'I'll be right back.'

She marched out into the corridor. Gavin was leaning against the wall, his head lowered.

'Okay, Gavin. I want an explanation right now. I thought Matthew was in your management team. You can't go giving dead arms to your team now, can you?'

Gavin shook his head. 'No, Miss.'

'I'm beginning to lose patience with you. I put my trust in you, and I hoped you'd repay it. I need to know what's going on.'

Gavin didn't look up. 'He said he can't go to the meeting at lunchtime.'

'Today?'

'Yes, Miss.'

'Do you know why he can't go to the meeting?'

'Because he has to go home, Miss?'

'That's right.' She paused, balancing her judgment. Half of her wanted to send Gavin back into the ranks, but that would destroy his confidence and probably cause lasting damage. The other half wanted to let him in on teacher-only knowledge, but if it got out that Matthew's mother was in the hospital, she could be in trouble with Greg. She'd only been working at Brentwell Primary for a few weeks: her job was hardly secure.

'I think we need to do some management team bonding,' she said at last. 'I think it's all very well getting the mums to make cakes for the stall, but how about we make a few ourselves?'

'What?'

'I have a friend who's a bit of a whizz in the kitchen. I'm sure she wouldn't mind coming in for a couple of cooking classes.'

Gavin shrugged. 'Sure, Miss.'

'Right. You wait here. I'm going to call Matthew outside, and I want you to apologise.'

Gavin just nodded. Jennifer suppressed a sigh and went back into the classroom. She waved Matthew from his seat and the little boy followed her outside.

'Gavin … what do you say?'

Gavin looked up. 'Sorry,' he mumbled.

Matthew smiled. 'Don't worry about it.'

'I wasn't really going to give you a dead arm,' Gavin said.

Matthew shrugged. 'It's all right.'

'You can go back inside, Matthew,' Jennifer said, opening the door. After Matthew had gone back into the classroom, she closed the door again and squatted down next to Gavin. The ghosts of classrooms past came back to haunt her, and she remembered the words of a million teachers she'd heard, overheard, seen on TV, read about, and had indoctrinated into her over her brief career:

This is your last chance.
I won't tell you again.
One more time and you're off the team.

I'll send a note home to your mother.

And she felt a wave of change ripple through her, and another voice rising, speaking up from the crowd:

Say something else.

Jennifer leaned down, and patted Gavin on the back, and smiled. 'You're a good boy, Gavin,' she said, tears in her eyes. 'I like you. You're going to do a good job of this, but let's keep a lid on the aggression, shall we? No use getting angry over a few cakes.'

Gavin looked up and nodded. Jennifer saw tears in his eyes too.

22

ACTIVISM

'I'M REALLY SORRY,' Jennifer said. 'I should have asked you first, but it was a spur of the moment thing.'

Angela chuckled. 'It would be an absolute delight. Do you want me to come into the school or would you like to bring the children here? Mondays and Tuesdays I'm free, but of course business is dying down a little bit, so it wouldn't hurt to shut the café for a morning or an afternoon.'

'I was thinking we could do a practice maybe this Friday, then another go next Wednesday, so that the cakes we made would be okay to sell at the festival.'

Angela clicked her fingers. 'Absolutely. Could ask the parents if it would be okay for me to take a few pictures to make a display for the wall in here? I think it would look nice next to the door.'

'Sure.'

'And have you cleared it with your school?'

Jennifer narrowed her eyes. 'Mr. Downton was only too pleased when I mentioned your name. He said he might stop by and have a look. Is there something you should be telling me?'

Angela shrugged. 'Oh, nothing. A charming man. I hope he stops by again soon. Sit down, I have something I'd like you to test for me.'

Jennifer grimaced as Angela went back into the kitchen, humming under her breath, practically skipping along as though she had not a care in the world. When she returned, she was carrying two huge mugs of steaming coffee.

'This is a new potion of my own construction,' she said, producing a can of instant whipped cream from a countertop. 'Maple and walnut latte with cinnamon cream.'

Jennifer watched, her stomach rumbling as Angela covered the drinks in a delicate swirl of cream, then pressed two brown marshmallows into the mixture and then stuck a chocolate flake in the top. A final dusting of icing sugar, and she presented the drink to Jennifer.

'These are naturally made hazelnut marshmallows I got from a shop in the Lake District,' she said. 'And this is an organic chocolate stick from the Eden Project in Cornwall. The marshmallows represent the falling autumn nuts, the chocolate is a leafless tree, and the icing sugar is the dusting of the first snow.' She gave a light, airy laugh. 'The cream is from Tesco. For the real thing, I'll whip up my own that I get from a local dairy.'

'Isn't that a bit too much snow?'

'I'll put a bit of chocolate food colouring in it to make it look like a forest floor. What do you think?'

Jennifer just shook her head. 'It's magnificent.'

Angela giggled. 'Thank you.'

'Do you do a low sugar version?'

'Absolutely not.'

Jennifer smiled. 'Then I'll have to get up early tomorrow and do some jogging.'

'Nothing like a bit of exercise, is there?'

JENNIFER DIDN'T QUITE MANAGE the jogging, but the next morning was a cold but beautiful clear day, so she got up earlier than usual, took Bonky for a walk up and down Willis Lane, then walked to work through Sycamore Park. It was quiet apart from a couple of dog walkers and a few solo joggers, but as she came around the eastern path to Big Gerry's courtyard, a council van was just pulling up. Jennifer stopped to watch as three men got out, carrying boxes of tools and ladders with them. They began to measure Big Gerry's trunk, then used torches to peer into cracks and fissures that had appeared over the years. Jennifer wandered a little closer and caught the eye of one of the men.

'What are you doing?' she asked.

The man gave her a grim smile. 'We're measuring the old boy up for surgery,' he said.

'What kind of surgery?'

'That remains to be seen.'

'You can't cut this tree down.'

The man sighed. 'Miss, when I was a boy, I used to climb up there with my mates and monkey about. We had great times. You could get right up if no one was looking, although my mum—god bless her—would have gone spare if she'd found out. These days, kids spend all their time staring at lumps of plastic in their hands. It's a real shame. Do you really think anyone except a few people my age would care if this tree got lopped down? A terrible shame it would be for sure.'

'It's a beautiful tree. You have to save it.'

'I'm not sure we'll have a choice, once they've had their vote up at the council.'

'When is it?'

'Next Thursday. And even worse will be if Clover gets her waterworks. Ruin the park forever that will.' The man smiled. 'Don't you worry, they'll never pass it. They can't.'

He said the last with a regretful uncertainty. Jennifer stared at Big Gerry for a moment longer, then checked her watch and bade the man a hasty farewell.

'ARE you sure this is a good idea?' Amy said, leaning over the copier as sheets of paper reamed out. 'Ringo's going to go off his nut if he finds out.'

'Ringo?'

Amy chuckled. 'Downton Abbey … Abbey Road … the Beatles. Get it?'

'Ah, sure. Now, can you go and check he's still in with Maud?'

'Okay, wait a minute.'

Amy sauntered off through the staffroom front door into the corridor, just as Rick came stumping in through the back. He looked at the stack of photocopies on the copier tray, then raised an eyebrow at Jennifer.

'Trying to lose your job?'

Jennifer narrowed her eyes. 'I have passion,' she said. 'And I have drive. Who would fire me?'

Rick smirked. 'Having a license doesn't mean you can drive, and I'm yet to see any evidence of passion. But, if you want to come over to mine this weekend, I'd be willing to give you an interview.'

'Will your other woman be there? The one I spoke to on the phone?'

Rick's face flushed so quickly it was as though Jennifer had slapped him. 'What are you talking about?'

'Your—'

'Quick! He's coming!' Amy shouted, as she ran back into the staffroom, crashing into a printer near the front and nearly knocking it off its table. As she turned to right it, her sleeve caught on a jar of pens on the edge of Downton's desk, sending them clattering to the floor. As the headmaster stepped into the room, looming over Amy, Jennifer jabbed at the copier's reset button, trying to get the print run to stop early. As the last sheet jetted out, she grabbed the cluster of prints and tried to stuff them into her desk drawer, only to trip on Rick's crutch.

'Watch where you're going,' he said, as two hundred sheets of paper plumed like confetti, then spread out across the desks and the floor, covering everything in requests to lobby the local council over the proposed waterworks and cutting down of Big Gerry, signed by Headmaster Greg Downton.

'What's this?' Downton said, picking up a sheet of paper that had landed with a corner in Old Don's half full coffee mug, collecting a grey-brown skin of gunk for its troubles. Downton's eyes narrowed, then he looked up at Jennifer.

'My office. Now.'

Jennifer closed her eyes. Through a haze of frustration, she heard Amy crying, and Rick offering her a new job as a live-in concubine.

She didn't really open her eyes until Downton's door had closed and the creak of his leather chair came from across his large, oak desk. He was sitting there, one leg over the other, peering at the letter through his glasses, frowning as though the type was still too small to read.

'You've got two on each page,' he said, not looking up.

'I thought I'd cut them in half to use less paper,' Jennifer croaked. 'Save the school some money—'

'Yes, yes.' Downton waved a hand. 'You've done a decent job of forging my signature.'

'I scanned it from another letter, and pasted it in as a Jpeg.'

Downton looked up, his eyes narrowed behind his glasses. 'Perhaps you'd be better suited to working in computer programming. I'm sure they have courses you can take in Belmarsh. You do know this is fraud? That I could have you arrested for identity theft, and not only would you never work as a teacher again, but you would probably get at least twenty years in maximum security, solitary confinement. If you were lucky. Do you understand?'

'Yes.'

Downton chuckled. 'However, I don't think it's necessary to go that far. Jennifer, your heart's in the right place, but you're a total idiot sometimes. Why on earth didn't you wait until I was out on business? Or just ask?'

'Because I didn't think you'd agree.'

'I actually feel it's quite a noble cause. That tree has stood for a thousand years—'

'About three hundred.'

Downton shrugged. 'Once you're past living memory, it doesn't matter that much, does it?'

'It's the fourth oldest sycamore in the UK.'

'Who cares? It's old, that's all that matters. If you'd asked, I'd have let you put a message on the school website. You know most of those letters won't ever make it home, don't you? They'll either get made into planes and tossed at the back of Old Don's head, or left to sit screwed up at the bottom of schoolbags for all eternity.'

'I have to do something.'

'I understand. So, send out your letters, and let's hope they make a difference.'

'So you're not going to fire me?'

Downton narrowed his eyes. 'You were our only applicant for Mrs. Goldsmith's position. If I fire you, I'd have to teach that unruly lot myself until we found someone else, and that's not going to happen.'

'Thank you.'

He leaned forward. 'But, you can do me a favour in return for my leniency.'

'Uh … what?'

Downton grimaced, then chuckled a little. He made a steeple with his fingers in front of him on the desk. 'So, this friend of yours, Angela Dawson. Does she ever mention me?'

23

TAKEAWAY NIGHT

IN THE END, they settled for an online petition. 'Don't tell Maud or I'll get an earful about budgets,' Downton said, instructing Jennifer to print out another ream of letters with a few of his ordered corrections. 'Just shred these. Perhaps you could get a class hamster or forty, to make use of all the bedding?'

'Let's get the harvest festival out of the way first,' Jennifer said. 'By the way, is it okay if I get off an hour early this afternoon, straight after the buses?'

'Why?'

'I want to visit Matthew Bridges' mum in hospital.'

'Oh, right. Sure. How is she?'

'I don't know, but it's not good.'

'Go right ahead. Give her my best.'

AS SHE WALKED BACK through Sycamore Park, Jennifer couldn't help but feel the weight of the world on her shoulders. Matthew Bridges' mother had been more ill than she had realised. At the weekend the poor woman was due to have a major operation, one which only had a fifty percent chance of success. There was every possibility that next week she could be dealing with a bereaved child. Remaining positive, however, she had insisted that Matthew continue to be involved with the harvest festival preparations, to take his mind off things, if nothing else. In order to ensure that things ran smoothly, she had decided to take Gavin Gordon into her confidence. Only time would tell whether that was a good idea or not, but she had trod the tightrope above the unemployment abyss for so long that she was wondering if it might be glued to her feet.

'Hey.'

Jennifer jumped as she turned around. Tom, wearing a deer-stalker hat which looked too big even for a man of his size, stood up from behind a bush.

'You have quite the talent for surprising me,' Jennifer said.

'I was just doing some pruning,' Tom said. 'Honestly, the excitement in my life never ends. Sometimes I think I'm so interesting I might just explode.'

'I hope not,' Jennifer said.

'Really?'

'I mean, I might get hit by that hat of yours. Where on earth did you get it?'

'I found a bear wandering around, so I caught it, skinned it, and made it into this hat.' He spread his arms. 'And the park became safe.'

'Are you sure?'

Tom grinned. 'No. My gran gave it to me for Christmas last year. She picked 3XL by mistake. Honestly, I didn't realise hats actually had sizes, or that you could get a triple X-sized head.'

'You can on the internet.'

'There's the truth right there.' Tom pulled off the hat, letting the wind immediately get to work on his hair. 'Um, are you busy?'

'Do you mean right now or in general?'

'Well, both.'

'No and yes.'

'That's good and bad. Let's just focus on the now. I didn't eat dinner yet, so if you also didn't eat dinner yet, perhaps we could somehow find ourselves eating dinner in the same place?'

Jennifer stared at him. The voices had started up again, one telling her to just drag him into the bushes, another that she needed to remain celibate and alone as long as possible in order to consider herself healed, and another that it wouldn't hurt to just eat dinner in his company, bearing in mind that eating was something she would need to do at some point, her stomach already grumbling.

However, there was always a stumbling block.

'I need to walk my dog,' she said.

Tom grinned. 'In that case, I've got a great idea,' he said. 'How about this? I walk your dog down to the nearest pub, leave it tied up outside while I have a pint, and in the meantime you cook me dinner. When you're ready, you can call a taxi to pick me up, and then walk down to get your dog while I sit on your sofa and watch TV?'

Jennifer tilted her head. 'Um, are you serious?'

Tom laughed. 'No, of course, not. I love dogs. Let's walk him together then pick up some cheap takeaway befitting our twin statuses of teacher and gardener. I know a Chinese place which almost certainly uses yesterday's grease, or a fish n' chips shop which does two-for-one after seven p.m. on weeknights. And to prove I'm not trying to weasel my way into your house, we can sit on the pavement outside to eat, or even walk up here, find a sheltered bench, and eat under the streetlights.'

'It sounds like the height of romance.'

'Even better if it's raining.'

Jennifer smiled. 'All right, why not?'

They headed for hers to pick up Bonky. Jennifer felt a little tingle of excitement as she walked alongside Tom, talking easily about nothing. When they reached her flat, she turned to Tom and said, 'You can come up, just while I get Bonky's lead. Don't mind the mess. It's normal.'

'You should see my place. Looks like one giant washing machine drum.'

Bonky started yapping at her feet as soon as she opened the door. Recognising Tom, the dog gave his ankles a rapid circuit, before continuing to badger Jennifer. Jumping down from the sofa, James came sauntering over, ignored Jennifer completely and began rubbing Tom's legs.

'Oh, I forgot you said you have a cat. I love cats.'

'Don't pick him up, he hates it—'

Too late, Tom had scooped James up into his arms, and the old cat flopped against his shoulder, head resting in the crux between Tom's shoulder and ear, for all intents and purposes a furry baby. His purring was so loud it could be heard even over Bonky's relentless whine.

'What a sweetheart,' Tom said, gently stroking James's back. 'I wish I still had a cat. I haven't had one since I was a kid, though. I've befriended most of the strays around Sycamore Park but I'm technically not allowed to feed them. I have to take them for neutering to keep the population down.' He grinned. 'Every time I spot a litter of kittens I bring them into the shack, domesticate them and pass them off to the local old ladies. Let me know if you need a couple more. There's always a litter or two in the spring.'

Jennifer couldn't help but shake her head. 'I knew you liked animals, but I never took you for a cat lady.'

'We had five while I was growing up. A couple of dogs too. And a chinchilla, which used to live freely around the house. All the cats and dogs were scared of it. You remember that Tom and Jerry cartoon where Jerry dresses the elephant up as a giant mouse?'

'I think so, yeah.'

'My parents loved pets, bless their hearts. They've both passed on now. And I'm too busy with the park to really take on a pet full time. I do have a few goldfish, though.'

'Do they all have names?'

Tom smiled. 'Of course. Now, if I can put this baby down for a while, we can walk Bonky down to the chip shop. It'll be just past seven by the time we get there. Or would you prefer greasy Chinese food?'

'Are they close?'

'Across the street.'

'Why don't we get chips from one, and greasy noodles from the other, and double down?'

'Sounds like a plan.'

James reluctantly allowed Tom to put him back on the sofa. They headed out with Bonky down to the two local takeaways, both at the far end of Willis Lane. Jennifer, who always headed through Sycamore Park, hadn't explored this part of town much, but found there was a cluster of decent shops and pubs around the junction with the main road heading into town.

They picked up the food and headed back. When they got to Jennifer's building, Tom sat down on the pavement.

'I'll wait here while you take Bonky inside,' he said.

Jennifer smiled. 'There's no way I could let James miss out on another couple of hours of stroking,' she said. 'However, it's a school night….'

'And a work night,' Tom said. 'I've got it. Don't worry, I'm a perfect gentleman.'

Jennifer's heart was fluttering. A significant part of her was hoping he wasn't quite perfect, even if she really needed an early night.

James, though, demanded a monopoly on Tom, taking up residence on Tom's lap the moment he sat down, then making himself comfortable for the night. Tom grimaced awkwardly as Jennifer passed him a plate of food, laughing as James woke up just long enough to take interest.

'Will he eat a prawn?'

'No, he'll just lick it a bit, so I wouldn't bother.'

'No problem. So, tell me, how was your day? I want to hear the real version, not the glossy, for-the-cameras version.'

Jennifer smiled. 'Do you really want to hear about my problems?'

Tom leaned forward as best he could over the relaxing ball of cat. 'Every single one,' he said. 'And if there's anything I can do to help, you only have to ask.'

'You're a very good actor,' Jennifer said.

Tom laughed. 'I can't be that good,' he said. 'I haven't been recognised in years.'

'I imagine the deer stalkers help with that,' Jennifer said.

'I own quite a collection. Nothing is as embarrassing as having an old dear stop you on the street. So, that's enough about me and my fame. If you want to know more, last time I looked I had a Wikipedia page. Tell me about you.'

Jennifer stared at him. She thought about the years she was together with Mark and tried to remember a time when he had ever asked her about herself. There had been the odd passing comment, but she couldn't remember him ever looking in her eyes with such sincerity as she saw in

Tom's. Before she knew it, tears had filled her eyes and she was covering her mouth to prevent herself from openly sobbing.

Tom frowned. 'He was a real dickhead, wasn't he? It's all right.'

Jennifer just nodded. 'I'm okay.'

'It's all right to cry, Jennifer.' Tom smiled. 'I'd come over and comfort you but I'm afraid the cat might try to rip my face off.'

24

SURPRISING DISCOVERIES

When she woke up on Thursday morning, Jennifer wanted to text Tom to apologise for basically complaining about her past for two hours before he finally admitted he ought to get going, but he had dropped another surprise on her by saying that he didn't own a phone. Instead, she lay in bed a little longer than she had intended, wondering whether she had unintentionally friend-zoned herself by spilling her frustrations on the past rather than her plans for the future. Tom, to his eternal credit, had listened intently, hands gentling massaging a purring James once he had finished eating. Jennifer, having opened the floodgates, was unable to stop until she'd bashed Mark into the ground like a disliked tent peg.

Getting up, she hastily walked Bonky down to the end of Willis Lane and back, before jumping into the car and making it to work with moments to spare before the morning meeting.

At lunchtime, she pulled Gavin Gordon aside.

'I need to tell you something important,' she said.

'What is it, Miss?'

'It's about Matthew. Well, about his mother. This is top secret, and you mustn't share it with anyone or I'll get into trouble with the headmaster. Please don't say anything to Matthew either.'

'Sure, Miss.'

'Matthew's mother is very sick. She's having a big operation this weekend and ah….'

'She might die?'

'I didn't say that—'

'But she might? What's her survival rate? Fifty percent?'

'Ah, she's very poorly.'

Gavin gave a sage nod. 'That sucks, Miss.'

'Yes, it does. It sucks very much. So I need you to be extra nice to Matthew. No threatening him with dead arms, no throwing his pens on the floor, no calling him a flid or a pindick.'

Gavin sniggered, then slapped a hand over his mouth, his face turning grave again. 'Sorry, Miss. It's just, you can't say that.'

'I know. That's why this conversation is secret. I don't want you to give him any special treatment, just be kind to him. That's all. I'm trusting you, Gavin. Don't let me down.'

Gavin stared at his hands for a long time. When he looked up, he frowned, then shook his head. 'Do you reckon he'd be up for seeing Argyle this weekend?'

'Probably best not to make him feel any worse.'

'We've got Liverpool at home in the Cup.'

'Well, at least he should see some goals. I don't know, you could ask him. Remember what I said, though. Not a word about his mother. Please.'

'Sure, Miss.'

'I mean it.'

'Okay, Miss.'

IN THE STAFFROOM, Rick was sitting with his casted foot up on a chair while Amy made him coffee.

'Ah, can you put just a little more sugar in, please, Clair? Not a whole spoonful, just like a quarter.'

'Sure.'

Jennifer rolled her eyes. 'Perhaps we could drop you off at the care home on the way home.'

Rick grinned. 'I have to rest up,' he said. 'The cast comes off tomorrow. The last thing I need is to give it a knock and end up with this beauty for another week.'

'What a shame that would be.'

Rick cupped a hand to his ear. 'Wait, can you hear that?'

Amy frowned. 'Is it a sparrow?'

Rick rolled his eyes. 'No, Clair. It's the sound of all the eligible ladies in Brentwell crying with disappointment.'

'There can't be that many, because I couldn't hear anything,' Jennifer said.

'That's because you're facing the playground,' Rick said. 'Too much background noise.'

'How about the one at home?' Jennifer said. 'Your girl-friend, or is it your wife?'

Rick glanced at Amy before giving a vehement shake of his head. 'I don't know what you're talking about.'

'The one I spoke to on the phone, who said you were still in bed.'

'That was me putting on a voice to confuse you.'

'It didn't sound like you.'

Rick gave a dramatic sigh. 'It was probably my sister, then.'

'You told me you were an only child,' Amy said.

Rick stood up. 'I don't have time for this,' he said. 'Some of us have work to do. Idle gossip will get you nowhere, ladies.'

'Looks like your leg's feeling better,' Jennifer said.

Rick looked down at the cast he was balancing on, then suddenly his face screwed up and he slumped back into the chair. 'Oh, the pain, the pain! Clair, grab my crutches, won't you?'

ON THE WAY HOME, Jennifer decided to stop in at the town museum and have a word with Gavin's mother, to see how he was getting on at home. It had rained in the morning so she had driven to work, however, after parking in the Pay & Display and walking through town, she found that the museum shut early on Thursdays. On the way back to the car park, she had to walk past the council building. It was nearly six o'clock, but a few lights were on in the upper floor windows. Perhaps Regina Clover was still at work?

Like a barbed wire fence, it was unlikely the woman would be swayed by gentle persuasion, but if Jennifer could spin a good enough sob story she might find a crack in the woman's iron-like defenses. She went inside, filled out a form at the reception desk, then was directed up the stairs to an office on the third floor.

She gave a light knock on the door, but no one answered. After another unanswered knock, she gently opened the door and peered inside. The room was small, made smaller by tall filing cabinets along the walls and folders of paperwork on every available surface. A desk stood in the middle of the chaos, a grey plateau among towering, snowcapped mountains. A couple of nodding solar powered dog ornaments sat among pots of pens, boxes of staplers and labels, and a cup that badly needed washing. The chair was on Jennifer's side, a computer in the desk's centre. Jennifer blinked as a screensaver suddenly appeared. At first she thought it was an actual video feed, before realising it repeated on a five second loop.

A sudden plan formulated in her mind, and she backed out of the room, closing the door behind her.

As she walked back down the corridor, she heard a toilet flush. She had just reached the top of the stairs when Regina Clover appeared out of a side door, hands shaking droplets of water over the floor. She didn't see Jennifer as she headed up the corridor and went into her office.

Jennifer hurried down the stairs and went to look for Tom. However, by the time she had got home, got the lead on Bonky and headed up to Sycamore Park with the dog in tow, Tom's shack was closed and he had gone home.

She went over to the Oak Leaf Café to ask Angela, but her friend just shook her head. 'I think he has rehearsal on a Thursday,' she said. 'Is it urgent?'

'Not so much, just a kind of madcap idea I had. It'll wait until tomorrow.'

'Have you eaten yet?'

Jennifer sighed. 'I don't have time to eat.'

'Oh, that's good news. I made this new quiche this afternoon, and really need someone to test it on before it goes live to the public. Are you happy to risk possible poisoning for a potentially exquisite dining experience?'

Jennifer smiled. 'I'll take the risk,' she said.

'Ah, but could you do me a favour?'

'Sure.'

'I've got a booking at eight for a family with a couple of kids, and I've run out of milk. Any chance you could run up to the supermarket and grab me some? You can leave Bonky here with me. I'll fix him something to eat.'

'You want me to literally run?'

Angela laughed. 'No, no, of course not. Actually, you could borrow my bicycle. It has a light and everything.' She reached into her pocket and produced a padlock key. 'It's around the back. Do you want me to show you?'

'It's okay. Just the milk?'

'Oh, and a bottle of wine, if you have the time. You can choose. Surprise me.'

Jennifer swapped the key for Bonky's lead, then went outside. It was just starting to get dark, but she found the bike chained up around the back of the café easily enough. It was a huge, powerful town bike with a sticker on the frame which said AMSTERDAM ORIGINAL. Angela had decorated the basket on the front with several plastic flowers in autumn colours, weaving their stems into the wire mesh.

The nearest supermarket was a ten-minute ride. As Jennifer whizzed through the streets, she considered down-grading her little car to a bicycle. Perhaps she could get a similar one to this and together they could go riding along the local cycle paths to view the autumn leaves.

She chained the bike up outside the supermarket and went inside. It was quiet at this time of night, most of the evening's commuters having already passed through. Jennifer wandered down a central aisle towards the refrigerated section, guiltily checking out the cakes on display in a confectionary area. She was almost there when a familiar voice drifted over from the adjacent aisle, freezing her to the spot.

'So, just honey-cured ham and we're done?'

'Unless you'd like something else in your sandwiches?'

'No, that would be great. Put a bit more mustard on, though.'

'I didn't want to make you sneeze.'

'It's okay.'

Accompanying the voices was a regular thump-thump-thump and a creak of something metallic. Jennifer shrank back behind a protruding rack of sale items as the owners of the two voices reached the end of the adjacent aisle and turned across the front of hers.

'Eric, can we have a look at the cheeses, too?' came the woman's voice, as Rick Fellow, crutchless, stumping along on his cast, appeared, pushing an older woman in a wheel-chair. From the shape of her face and even the curls in her hair, this was clearly his mother.

Jennifer stared as they passed, not seeing her.

'Eric,' the woman said as Rick gave a gentle sigh, reaching back to pat him on the arm. 'Eric, just pause by the camembert a second so I can see if any is on sale.'

'It gives me wind, Mum.'

'I know, dear, but that's a good thing, isn't it? It means there's nothing stuck.'

25

STAR TURN

'HE'S HAD A HAIRCUT,' Amy whispered, leaning close to Jennifer, still absently sharpening a pencil crayon. 'Why do you think that is?'

Greg Downton, hair freshly cut and gleaming with a hint of replenished colour, stood up. 'Okay, everyone, thanks for staying awake. This is our last meeting of the week. We have just one week left until the harvest festival. Please make sure you've got everything ready for your class. We don't have much time left. We'll be setting up the stalls next Thursday night, so keep your evening clear. Any questions?'

Amy shot up a hand.

'Don't ask him,' Jennifer hissed.

'Uh, Mr. Downton … could I just ask—' She shot a grin at Jennifer, '—whether another letter will go out to parents to confirm the details?'

'Yes, Ms. Clairmont. It will. Of course it will.'

'Thanks.'

The staffroom's rear door opened and Rick came in, a bag slung over his shoulder, but the cast gone. He winced as he made an exaggerated limp towards his desk, then sat down with a sigh and a grimace.

'Good of you to join us, Mr. Fellow,' Downton said.

'I had an early appointment at the doctor,' Rick said. 'He said it might have been a few days too early to remove the cast, but I'm a tough one.' He lifted a hand and made a fist. Amy giggled. Old Don rolled his eyes and muttered 'pillock,' just a little too loud.

'Well, that's good to know,' Downton said. 'Right, everyone, have a good day.'

'You girls miss me this morning?' Rick asked, leaning forward. 'Looks like you were crying. Your makeup's running.'

Amy immediately pulled open her top drawer and took out a little vanity mirror. Jennifer just smiled. 'Must be nice to be off the crutches,' she said as Rick opened his bag and took out a lunchbox which he put into his middle desk drawer.

'What's for lunch today? Ham or camembert?'

Before Rick could reply, Jennifer scooped up a pile of maths books and hurried off to class.

'Miss, can I have a word?'

'Sure, Gavin. What is it?'

Just in case his mouth ran away from him, Jennifer took Gavin out into the corridor, leaving the other children watching a DVD on the Roman Empire.

'Miss, can I show you something? It's in my bag.'

'Sure, go and get it.'

Gavin ran off to the cloakroom, then came back a minute later carrying his schoolbag. He opened it and pulled out a large piece of folded card, slightly crumpled.

'I made this,' he said, holding it out to her.

Jennifer stared. Crudely illustrated in Gavin's distinctive barely legible style, it was a picture of a woman—presumably—sitting in a chair with her arms raised, while around her, smaller figures—presumably children—also had their arms raised. Above the group, circles of colour with trailing lines that sometimes touched represented balloons. Along the top Gavin had written *Mat's Mum*, and on the bottom, *Get Well Soon*.

'I was thinking to pass it round on Monday,' Gavin said. 'Obviously if she snuffs it, I'll have to make another one. What do you think?'

Jennifer wanted to point out that Matt had two Ts, but the lump in her throat suddenly exploded, and all she could do was start to cry.

'It's perfect,' she choked, trying not to be sick. 'Just perfect.'

~

TOM, wearing waders, was standing up to his thighs halfway across the duck pond, poking at something with a stick. When Jennifer called his name he turned and gave her a wave.

'Just unblocking the fountain,' he said. 'I'll be there in a minute.'

A few minutes later, with the newly unblocked fountain bubbling gently away in the middle of the pond, Tom emerged onto dry land and began stripping off his waders.

'Been meaning to get to that for ages,' he said. 'I wasn't sure it would even still work. Now it's going again, it should clear the water a little so you can see the fish better.'

'I need a favour,' Jennifer said.

'Sure.'

'I need you to come with me to talk to Regina Clover.'

'I think I'd rather dive straight back into the pond,' Tom said. 'Why?'

'I've thought of a way to both save Big Gerry, and prevent the new water treatment plant,' Jennifer said. 'And I think you hold the key to both.'

Tom grimaced. 'I'm not going to … you know, if that's what you mean. She must be about eighty-five.'

'You won't have to. At least I hope not.'

Tom looked awkward. 'Can't I just stay here and rake leaves? It's so much easier.' His eyes brightened. 'Oh. We've got a couple of hedgehogs preparing for hibernation. Any chance you could bring your class down for a fieldtrip next week?'

'Actually, I'm bringing them to Angela's café on Tuesday for a cooking class. We decided against doing it in the school because Angela was worried she might forget something. I'm sure we could find time for a guided tour.'

'Great. I'd love to show them the hedgehogs.'

Jennifer gave him a light punch on the arm. 'So … Regina. If we're quick we can make it this afternoon, before the council offices close.'

Tom sighed. 'All right, come on then. I can drive.'

Twenty minutes later, they pulled up outside the council offices. Only when they were in Tom's car had Jennifer realised he still smelled of pond, but it was too late to do anything about it now. Together, they headed inside.

They signed in at the reception and headed up the stairs. Jennifer knocked on Regina's door and this time received a sharp, 'Who is it?'

'My name is Jennifer Stevens, from Brentwell Primary,' Jennifer said. 'I'm here with a friend, Tom, who works as the caretaker in Sycamore Park. Could we please have a word?'

There was a long pause. Jennifer glanced at Tom, who shrugged. 'Give her a chance to change out of her witch's costume,' he whispered.

'All right. You get two minutes,' came Regina's voice.

Jennifer clenched a fist, then grinned at Tom, who just shrugged again. Straightening her blouse, and giving her hair a quick pat, Jennifer opened the door.

Regina was sitting behind her desk, writing something on a piece of paper. She didn't even look up as they entered.

'I hope you're not planning some stupid protest,' she said, still leaning over her work. 'You can chain yourself to whatever you want, but if you think I'll make you a cup of tea, you can get stuffed.'

Jennifer was about to speak when the screensaver came up on Regina's computer monitor. Jennifer glanced up at Tom who had a big grin on his face. She had told him about it in the car, but he hadn't believed her. Facing them was an advertisement for a West End production of Les Misérables, with Tom's character, poised to begin a song, in the middle of the screen. As Jennifer gave Tom a nudge in the ribs, he spread his arms, and sung in a deep baritone, 'We have come ... to save ... the park!'

Regina looked up, nearing falling out of her chair. Her glasses fell off her face, and she scrabbled to pick them up.

Tom was in full flow now, making up lines as he went along. 'The trees ... will last forever, and ever, while your smile is just a memoreeeeeeeee...!'

'Thomas J. Reynolds?' Regina cried, jumped up out of the chair. 'Is it really you?'

'I am ... heeeeeee,' Tom sang. Jennifer, her ears smarting, gave him another nudge.

'You can probably knock it off now.'

'Oh my God. I can't believe it!'

Tom gave a short bow. 'Since leaving the industry, I would like to thank you as a representative of the town council for my employment in Sycamore Park, and trust that you will continue to keep it as the wonderful place that it is, for the enjoyment of adults and children alike.'

Regina's eyes narrowed. She glanced from Tom to Jennifer. 'Is this some attempt at a bribe?'

Tom shook his head. 'Not much chance of that on a council salary,' he said, flashing a TV grin that had Regina giggling and Jennifer rolling her eyes. 'However, if you would be interested, I'd be happy to get you a backstage pass for my latest production at Brentwell Community Theatre. It's not exactly the Old Vic but it's fun. And in addition, I've got a small part in the panto this year. Do you know who's starring in that? Phillip Schofield. I could probably introduce you, if you like.'

'No!' Regina cried, her hands flying up in the air, making Jennifer wonder if she really did have some kind of witchy spell going on. 'I mean, yes! I'd love to! Oh, how fantastic!'

'Would you like me to sign something while I'm here? Or maybe a picture? Perhaps when Phil comes to town, we can get one together. We can probably rustle up a costume for you to wear.' As Regina, practically hyperventilating, dived into her bag for a camera, Tom glanced at Jennifer. 'There's usually a Grotbags one lying around somewhere,' he muttered under his breath.

'Good call on Philip Schofield,' Jennifer whispered.

'What woman in late middle age doesn't want to meet him?' Tom whispered back.

'Got it!' Regina said, holding up a camera like a diamond recovered from a swamp. 'We'll stand over there, by the door. You, you can take it. What was your name again?'

'Jennifer,' Jennifer said.

'That's nice. Well, make sure you get us at a good angle.' She squealed as Tom put an arm around her shoulders.

Jennifer held up the camera. 'Say tree,' she said.

26

PICNICS AND MOSAICS

TOM'S REQUEST in return for selling out his acting soul to save Big Gerry was for Jennifer to join him for a picnic on Sunday on the grassy knoll in the centre of Sycamore Park. With unseasonably warm weather due over the weekend, he said it might be their last chance. However, to make it clear that it definitely wasn't a date, he asked her to invite Angela along. Angela, of course, was delighted.

'Can I bring a friend?' she asked.

Jennifer shrugged. 'I don't see why not.'

'Great. Is it a pot luck party?'

'Uh … I don't know.'

'We all have to bring something, right?'

'I suppose so.'

'Great. I'll rustle a few things up in the morning, then have one of the part-timers cover a couple of hours over lunchtime.'

Angela, uncharacteristically, didn't invite Jennifer to stay for dinner on Friday night. She had done her hair, and kept checking in a wall mirror each time she passed.

'Are you expecting someone?' Jennifer said.

Angela just chuckled. 'Whatever gave you that idea?'

'Well, good luck with it. I'll see you on Sunday.'

SATURDAY WAS BRIGHT AND SUNNY. Jennifer did a little shopping therapy in the morning before walking Bonky around Sycamore Park in the afternoon. She picked up a coffee from Pete's stall on the way home, and was surprised to find him whistling to himself behind the counter.

'You're cheerful,' she said.

Pete shrugged. 'I just got a new commission,' he said.

'A commission?'

'To design a mosaic.'

'Oh, I remember Tom telling me. You're a part time artist, aren't you?'

Pete nodded. 'This one's a little bigger than anything I've been asked to do before,' he said. 'Should be fun.'

'I'm looking forward to seeing it,' Jennifer said.

It was looking like a beautiful evening, even though the chill was quickly closing in. Jennifer stared at the sky, the only cloud being the knowledge that Matthew Bridges' mother was going in for her operation tonight. They would know by Monday morning whether or not she would make it.

AT ELEVEN O'CLOCK on Sunday morning, Jennifer headed around to meet Tom, who had wanted to check a few things at his shack before the picnic started. She found him leaning over one of the hedgehog boxes, a wide grin on his face.

'Come over here,' he said. 'Listen. You can hear him shuffling about in there.'

Jennifer put her head to the wood and heard a rustling sound from inside the box. 'What's he doing?' she asked.

'Getting ready to hibernate,' Tom said.

'Isn't it a bit early?'

'Yeah, he won't go into full hibernation for a few weeks. He's just getting his bed ready.'

'I fancy the idea of hibernation,' Jennifer said.

'Ah, but you'd miss Christmas,' Tom said. 'We have a spectacular tree. And I'm thinking to ask my new best friend Regina Clover if we can have a Christmas festival.'

'I'm sure she'd agree if you serenade her again.'

Tom grimaced. 'Maybe. Are you ready for the picnic?'

Jennifer lifted a bag. 'Ham sandwiches, coffee, and a cake from Tesco. I'm hoping Angela will do most of the heavy lifting when it comes to food.'

'Good work. I've got corn soup in a flask, an apple pie I floundered through yesterday, and a box of sausages on sticks.'

Jennifer smiled. 'Then we're sorted. Let's go.'

Before she realised she was even doing it, Jennifer linked an arm through Tom's. He looked down, lifting an eyebrow. Jennifer just shrugged. Then together, they headed up the hill.

They found Angela already there, laying out a patch-work blanket behind the large rock feature at the top, a basket holding down one corner, a large cooler another, and stones placed on the other two. 'I figured we'd need a windbreak,' she said as they arrived, nodding at the rock feature. 'It's not quite as warm as I was hoping, but I think we'll get a good couple of hours. I brought a mixture of hot and cold food, so we're covered for all eventualities. Oh, look at that!' She began to laugh as the wind gusted suddenly, showering them with golden leaves. 'Catch one, quick! It's good luck.'

Jennifer snatched ungainly at a couple of fluttering leaves, before plucking one that had got stuck to Tom's coat. She held it up with a look of triumph.

'There you go,' Angela said. 'Everything will work out now.'

'You should have given me a shout,' Tom said. 'I'd have helped you carry your stuff.'

'Oh, it wasn't so far,' Angela said. 'And that cooler's just for the pies and cakes. My friend is bringing the wine.'

'Where is she?' Tom asked.

'Uh, he,' Angela said, giving a little chuckle.

Jennifer felt a sudden sinking feeling in her stomach. 'Um, please don't tell me it's—'

Too late, Angela stood up to wave at a figure walking up the hill, leaning beneath the weight of a carrier bag bulging with wine bottles. His identity wasn't immediately apparent beneath the unseasonal straw hat he was wearing, but from his gait Jennifer could tell.

'Ah, Greg! There you are!' Angela said, jumping up. She jogged over to Downton like a woman forty years younger, taking his arm and steering him towards the picnic mat.

In his straw hat, and with a pinstripe shirt above beige slacks just for good measure, Downton looked ready to go boating on the Thames circa 1950. The smile he gave Angela was filled with pure joy, so Jennifer felt rather like a party pooper when she saw the way it dropped as his eyes met hers.

'Oh, Ms. Stevens … ah, Jennifer. I wasn't expecting to see you here.'

'Likewise, Mr.… ah, Greg.'

'I'm Tom,' Tom said with a wide grin, jumping up and

reaching for Downton's hand. 'Lovely to meet you. I'm currently working as the caretaker of Sycamore Park, but just so you don't think I'm a total country bumpkin, I was also once in *EastEnders*.'

Downton just gaped, lost for words.

'Seriously?' Jennifer said, exchanging a glance with Angela who grinned and shrugged.

'Three episodes. I sold Phil Mitchell a stolen motor.' He pouted, then put on a frown and said in a perfect East End accent, '"You'd better pay up for that motor, or else." Ha, that was my favourite line.'

'And did he?' Downton asked.

Tom smiled. 'I don't remember. Maybe off-screen. I got cut from the budget.'

'Well, it's nice to meet you, too. In case you didn't know, I'm the headmaster at Brentwell Primary.' Downton glanced at Jennifer. 'Good to see you're settling in to the area, Ms. Stevens. Making things a little more permanent. It's so hard to find good teaching staff around here.'

'Um, thanks.' She glanced at Tom, who grinned and winked, then back at Downton. 'We're not … uh—'

'It's okay, I'll keep it quiet from the teaching staff. You do know how they like to gossip. And poor Fellow will be heartbroken.'

'Fellow?' Tom said.

'Mr. Fellow. Rick. He has a soft spot for Jennifer, I've been led to believe.'

'He'd have a soft spot for Maud if she was ten years younger,' Jennifer said.

'Well, quite, the young man does have a bit of an infatuation issue—'

'Anyone for pie?' Angela said with a wide grin, holding up a cake knife. Downton chuckled. Tom and Jennifer exchanged glances. The smile on Tom's face could have meant anything.

Once the initial awkwardness was over and they were all a couple of glasses of wine deep, Jennifer found herself coming to like the stern old headmaster. Angela in particular seemed enamoured, falling into hysterics at each of his terrible jokes, holding on to his every word as he recounted some past tale of school life.

'So my first position as a Deputy Head at a Secondary in Penzance, we had this teacher called Mr. Trovers, who was a bit of a pushover. The kids would run him ragged, putting pins on his chair, chalk on the door handles, that kind of thing. One time he was due to go into a particularly rough class, so I suggested he shove a piece of plywood down the back of his trousers. Well, he went in and sat down, and they had a test that day, see. So he's there at the front of the class feeling all smug because the board must have caught all the pins, and the kids are looking a bit confused as to why there's no reaction. Well, it turned out one of the kids' dads was a mechanic and this kid had stolen some industrial glue. When Trovers came to stand up, it turned out he was stuck fast to the seat. And the board down his arse had pulled his trousers so tight that we had to send the caretaker in to cut him out. Quite the chuckle we had over that one.'

Tom and Angela were crying with laughter. Jennifer pretended to be serious, but even she had a smile on her face.

'What happened to him in the end?' Jennifer asked.

'He went for a change of career,' Downton said. 'Last I heard, he was driving a coach for National Express.'

'Kids can be rough sometimes,' Tom said. 'We used to put worms in our form teacher's drawer.'

'They're like wolves,' Downton said. 'If they sense

blood, they'll rip you apart. Even the reception class. Devils in human form, every single one.'

'They're not all bad,' Jennifer said.

Downton smiled. 'I'd love to agree with you, but then I wouldn't be a good headmaster, would I? If the kids find out I'm a dragon that can't breathe fire, there'd be anarchy. I fully expect next week's harvest festival to turn into a zombie apocalypse.'

Angela patted him on the arm. 'I'll make sure to run a vegetarian menu that day,' she said. 'That should keep the zombie wolves from the door.'

'Good call.'

Tom stood up, frowning in the direction of the court-yard. 'What's going on down there?' he said. 'A van from the council just showed up. Hang on, I'll go and have a look.'

'I'll come with you,' Angela said. Then, turning back to Jennifer and Downton, she added, 'You two couldn't be loves and put the leftovers away, could you? It's starting to turn a little chilly and I think it might be a good idea to relocate to the café for the after party.'

As Tom and Angela headed off down the hill, Jennifer turned to Downton.

'So, um, ah, well … are you and Angela … a, um….'

'Out with it, Miss Stevens,' Downton snapped, glaring at her, before abruptly chuckling with laughter. 'Are you wondering if your friend and I are an item?'

'Well, yes?'

Downton sighed. 'You'd probably better ask her about that. We enjoy each other's company. We're both sepa-rated, and both getting a bit long in the tooth. And she's lovely, isn't she? Like a breath of fresh air in a dingy old room.'

'I suppose that's one way of putting it.'

'And you never know when your time might be up, do you? Might as well live a little before you die.'

Jennifer grimaced. 'Speaking of which … I don't suppose you've heard anything about Matthew Bridges' mum?'

Downton sighed. 'I called the hospital this morning, but there was nothing much they could tell me. She made it through the operation, but she was still under sedation when I called. The doctor told me they'd know later today whether she's likely to make it or not.'

'Poor Matthew. I can't imagine what he's going through.'

'You never really know how important someone is until they're gone, do you?'

Jennifer shook her head.

'I made the mistake with my Debbie. She left me for a pastry chef. Said I was boring, that my personality was as grey as my clothes. I only dressed that way because I thought it was befitting the job. If I'd known she wanted me to dress like a strawberry, I'd have gotten a job as a fireman. Do you think I'm boring, Stevens?'

Fearing that Downton had been a little too generous with refilling his own glass of wine, Jennifer just gave a shrug she hoped would cover all bases. She looked down the hill towards Tom, hoping to catch his eye.

'I mean, after she left me, I went through my wardrobe, and found that everything I owned filled the same spectrum on the colour scale, from light grey to black. It was sobering. So I went out and bought a lemon yellow shirt. I promised myself that I would never dress like an old Filofax again. Except for at work, when it's expected, but outside work it would be all greens and blues and oranges. Do you see where I'm coming from, Stevens?'

Help me, Jennifer mouthed in Tom's general direction,

and perhaps through some psychic link she hadn't previously realised existed, he turned and began to walk back up the hill.

To her surprise, both Tom and Angela were smiling. As they reached the picnic spot where neither Jennifer nor Downton had begun to do any tidying at all, Angela did a little skip, then reached down and took Downton's hands, pulling him to his feet.

'It appears Big Gerry's had a stay of execution,' she said, spinning him in a circle which nearly sent him crashing face first into the rock feature, 'and even better—they've cancelled the plans for the water treatment plant.'

Jennifer looked up at Tom and blinked. 'Really?'

Tom sat down beside her. 'Really. It looks like I sold my soul to Regina Clover in exchange for Big Gerry's continued survival.'

'I'm sure that if Big Gerry could talk, he would thank you in a big, booming tree-like voice,' Jennifer said.

Tom smiled. 'It was thanks to you,' he said. 'Had you not spotted the weak point, we would never have defeated the end-of-level boss.' His smile dropped. 'Seriously, you made a difference, Jennifer. You might have only lived here a couple of months, but that tree's been there forever. While there might not be anyone still alive—at least I hope not—who remembers when it was planted, there are plenty who remember it being a little smaller. This park means a lot to a lot of people, and you helped protect that.'

Jennifer wiped away a tear. 'Thank you for saying that, even if it's a little melodramatic.'

Tom leaned forward. 'Can I be a little bit more melodramatic before I turn back into the tough old gardener?'

'Um, sure.'

'How about me and you go out for a proper date tonight? Like, in a restaurant, or something?'

Jennifer opened her mouth to reply, but before she could say anything, Downton jumped, one hand flapping at his back.

'Ow! I think I just got stung by a bee. Aren't they supposed to be hibernating by now?'

'Oh, Greg,' Angela said, shaking her head as she loaded uneaten food back into her picnic basket. 'Don't be such a drama queen. It was probably just an ant.'

27

WINS AND LOSSES

WHILE THE WEEKEND forecast was for pleasant weather, on the Monday before the harvest festival, the wind was up as Jennifer made her way through Sycamore Park on the way to work, showers of leaves billowing around her as she clung on to her bag for dear life.

To her surprise, as she reached the southern end of the park, she found Angela standing beside a beaming Pete Markham on the edge of Big Gerry's courtyard while a group of council workers wandered around with tape measures and shovels.

'Good morning!' she called, although she was sure her voice was lost over the wind. She waved her hand instead, and Angela, wrapped in a thick duffel jacket, looked up and waved.

'Isn't it exciting?' she said, as Jennifer reached them.

'It's Monday morning,' Jennifer said. 'Neither of you are supposed to be working today, so why aren't you still at home in bed? It's freezing!' She turned to look at the council workers. 'What are they doing?'

'They're starting to re-lay the courtyard stones,' Pete

said, a wide grin on his face. 'They want to get it done in time for your school's harvest festival this weekend.' He held out a clipboard to reveal a complicated design of a tree with its branches spread. 'This is what it'll look like in the end. All natural stones and colours.'

'Oh, wow, it's beautiful. They're going to do that by this weekend?'

Pete shook his head. 'Unfortunately not. They're just flattening it for now. The full design will take a couple of months, but it should be done by Christmas. Big Gerry's getting the full light-up treatment this year, according to the revised plans.'

Angela was shaking her head. 'Who'd have thought Regina Clover would turn out to have such a kind heart? It defies all sense.'

Jennifer grinned. 'Well, it's fantastic news for both of you. As long as no one gets poisoned by my class's cakes, it'll all be good.'

Angela lifted an eyebrow. 'How could that possibly happen with a teacher as good as me?'

Jennifer smiled. 'My little zombie wolves are looking forward to it,' she said. 'Anyway, I'd better get to work. Both of you have a lovely day.'

She hurried off with a spring in her step, but as she reached the school gates, her feet began to feel a little more leaden. Greg Downton was standing on the steps outside the main entrance, and as their eyes met, he waved her over. Unsmiling, he requested for her to join him in his office.

'There's good and bad news, I'm afraid,' he said, sitting down behind his desk, unsmiling, leaving Jennifer standing, her heart thundering in her chest.

'Matthew's mum—?'

Downton gave a grim smile. 'She'll be absolutely fine. I

just had a call from the hospital. She's awake and aware and out of danger. She'll be kept in for a couple of weeks so unfortunately she's going to miss the harvest festival, but she'll be fine. Perhaps you could ask those demons of yours to make a doggy bag or something? And you can go ahead and tell that future criminal you put in charge that he can collect signatures for his sorry excuse for a card.' His smile widened just a fraction. 'And don't forget to have him bring it to me so I can add my own paw print to the mix. She's going to be fine, Jennifer. Just fine.'

Jennifer couldn't resist a little clench of her fist. If Downton had been standing, she might have hugged him, but instead she just bounced up and down a couple of times.

'That's fantastic,' she said at last. 'I'm so happy for Matthew. Um … you said there was bad news?'

Downton sighed and rubbed his head. 'I feel like death warmed up. How many times did you top up my damn wine, Stevens? I only remember having a couple of glasses.'

'Perhaps you're getting old, sir?'

Downton groaned. 'I'm only fifty-nine,' he muttered. 'Go on, get out of here, Stevens. You're on bus monitor duty, and those demon transports are due any minute.'

RICK WAS STANDING out by the edge of the car park, hands in his pockets, a beanie hat pulled over his head. As Jennifer reached him, he puffed his cheeks out against the cold.

'Why are you smiling? Pleased to see me?'

Jennifer laughed. 'Of course not. I just had some good news.'

'Well, it's lucky for some. I somehow failed to pull this weekend.'

'How tragic. The eligible young ladies of Brentwell had a lucky escape again?'

Rick shook his head. 'Nah. Mate and me we went clubbing in London. Honestly, like shooting fish in a barrel. I had five or six lined up, but my mate wanted to go home.'

'That's too bad.'

Jennifer chuckled to herself as the first of the buses pulled in and began to reverse into the parking spaces. Other kids were walking through the school gates, bags over their shoulders, hands in pockets.

'Wow, look at that muppet,' Rick said, nodding at one little boy who'd just come in through the gates. 'He's wearing an Argyle hat. Might as well put a sign on his head that says "Give me a kicking, please".'

'Don't be unkind,' Jennifer said, giving him a nudge in the ribs.

'And I don't know why he's looking so happy. They lost seven one.'

'Rick, just give it up,' Jennifer said. 'I know it's all an act. You're a nice guy, really.'

'Oh, bugger off.'

'You're the carer for your disabled mother, *Eric*,' she said. 'I saw you in the supermarket.'

Rick turned to glare at her. 'Tell no one,' he said. 'And knock off the "Eric" business.'

'What's wrong with it?'

'It's a loser's name.'

'Loads of cool famous people are called Eric.'

'Name one.'

'Well … oh, good morning, Matthew.'

'Good morning, Miss,' Matthew Bridges said, giving

his brand new Plymouth Argyle hat a nudge up above his eyes.

'That's a nice hat,' Jennifer said.

'Gav's dad got it for me,' Matthew said, beaming. 'We lost but it was a great game. That free kick that put us one nil up….' He swung a foot through the air. 'Pow!' He grinned again. 'Gav said he's going to come round and give me a few pointers. He reckons I could make it on the wing if I can learn to cross.'

'Gav?' Jennifer lifted an eyebrow. 'Are you two boys friends now?'

Matthew made a face. 'We're not *friends*, Miss. Only girls have friends. We're *mates*. Dad said Gav can come fishing with us on Sunday, after the festival.'

'That sounds great. How's your mum?'

Matthew nodded. 'She's great. We popped in to see her early this morning before school. She gave Dad a cake recipe to make for the festival since she'll still be in hospital.' Matthew sniggered. 'But I reckon he'll burn it. He can't even tell the difference between sugar and salt.'

'Oi, Matt!' came a sudden bellowing cry from across the playground. 'Get over here. We need one more for five-a-side!'

'Coming, Gav!'

Matthew dropped his schoolbag at Jennifer's feet and ran off to join the game. Jennifer watched him for a few seconds, then shrugged and bent down to pick up his bag.

'They'll lose anything that's not tied to them,' she said to Rick, who just puffed his cheeks out and shifted from foot to foot, shivering in the morning chill.

'So, are we mates or friends?' he said, giving her a sideways glance.

'We're work colleagues,' Jennifer said with a smile. 'But if you're brave enough to join me and Amy at an Argyle home game in a couple of weeks, I'll let you graduate to friend.'

Rick grimaced. 'Colleagues it is, then. I'd never be seen dead at an Argyle game.'

'Not even Argyle ladies?'

Rick stared at her a moment, then stuck a hand in his pocket and pulled out a small leather-bound diary. 'So, what day are we talking about, again?'

28

BAKING AND WILDLIFE SPOTTING

THE WIND WAS GETTING UP, sending leaves scattering across the duck pond. Behind his caretaker's shack, Tom squatted down beside one of the hedgehog boxes. With a smile, he turned to the gathered kids, some with hands in their pockets, other hopping from foot to foot against the chilly wind, a few with Disney-themed ear muffs pressing their hair to their heads.

'Okay, get as close as you can, and don't make too much noise. I don't want to startle him.'

'Can I pick it up?' Gavin said.

'Not unless you want a handful of needles,' Tom said. 'They're prickly little things.'

The kids keened forward. Jennifer, standing at the back, caught Tom's eye and gave him a smile. He smiled back, then lifted the wooden lid. The kids oohed and aahhed at something Jennifer couldn't quite see.

'Looks like he's asleep,' Tom said, lowering the box lid. 'Did you know, hedgehogs were originally called urchins, which is where the word sea urchin comes from?'

'Gavin's an urchin,' Paul Lemon quipped with a grunted laugh.

'Shut up, Lemons,' Gavin said.

'Yeah, shut up Lemons,' Matthew Bridges repeated.

'Boys!' Jennifer said, as a grinning Paul Lemon grabbed Gavin and Matthew around the shoulders and tried to launch himself into the air.

'My dad says you can keep them as pets,' Gavin said.

'My dad says they've all got rabies,' Paul said. 'He said you've got rabies, too.'

'Shut up, you turkey. My dad says your mum—'

'Okay!' Tom clapped his hands together. 'Who wants to see some pretty little squirrels?' As cheers and cries of 'Me! Me! Me!' drowned out Paul and Gavin's bickering, Tom said, 'We have a few living in a big sycamore just over there. If we put some nuts down, they might just come and have a look.'

As the kids charged off towards the tree, almost certainly scaring off any squirrels, Jennifer caught up with Tom.

'You'd make a good teacher,' she said, resisting the urge to pat him on the arm, aware of the interrogation she'd get from the kids if any of them spotted it.

He shrugged. 'I don't know what I'd teach,' he said. 'Weeding classes?'

'How about acting?' she said. 'You could do acting classes. After all, you were in *EastEnders*.'

'Three episodes,' Tom said. 'Funny how I spent six months as Hamlet in the Queens Theatre in Norwich yet when I die they'll write "Once told Phil Mitchell to pay up" on my headstone.'

'I bet you'd get loads of takers,' Jennifer said.

Tom shrugged. 'I'll think about it. By the way, I don't

recall ever getting an answer to my question from Sunday. The one about dinner—'

'Miss! Miss, quick! Paul fell in the pond!'

Jennifer frowned. 'Hang on a minute,' she said. Then, turning to the kids, she shouted, 'How did Paul end up in the pond? It's behind us?'

'He was chasing a rat,' Gavin said, as Paul, sodden and draped with dark green weed like some monstrous water creature, climbed out of the pond, shaking droplets of water in the general direction of several screaming girls.

'It's not a rat, it's a water vole,' Tom said. 'There's a family living in the riverbank. 'I call that one Monty. Please try not to scare him.'

'I'm coming to get you!' Paul roared at the girls, then broke into a sludgy run, throwing lumps of weed around while simultaneously howling with laughter.

'Would you like me to go and fetch some chains?' Tom asked, giving Jennifer a sideways smile.

LATER, with Paul Lemon now dressed in some overfitting clothes Tom had found lying around in the shack, the kids crowded around Angela's worktop. Angela, wearing an apron with a maple-leaf design in the middle, held up a bowl of sugar.

'This is sugar,' she said. 'And this over here is salt. A very important rule of cooking is to not mix them up.'

'My dad says salt comes from the sea,' Paul said.

'My dad says you came from the sea,' Gavin said, nudging Paul in the ribs. 'He said you got caught in a fishing net, but no zoo wanted you so they gave you to your mum and dad.'

'Seven one,' Paul replied.

'Shut up. The ref was blind.'

'Boys,' Jennifer said, patting both on the shoulder. 'Concentrate.'

The door opened and a man entered, a shy smile on his face. Jennifer wasn't sure who was more surprised to see Greg Downton, herself or the kids. One person who clearly wasn't surprised, however, was Angela, who looked up, gave Downton a warm smile, and then nodded to a side table.

'Ah, Greg, just in time. I'm about to split them into groups. You'll lead group two.' The kids sniggered at the use of Downton's first name. Angela was unconcerned as she waved at Jennifer and Tom. 'You guys will take group three, since you have less experience.'

'Less experience?'

As Downton went to his allocated table, Angela leaned over and whispered, 'Greg's a regular at an evening cookery class I teach. He's my best student.'

'You mean—'

Angela's eyebrows rose and she tilted her head. 'You didn't think I pulled him at a nightclub, did you? Although … I did know he would be there.'

Jennifer grimaced. 'There's so much I wish I could unhear right now,' she said, as Angela burst into singsong laughter.

'Ha, you're with the Pope,' one of the kids said to another, just a little too loud.

'Yeah, but at least I'm not with Miss and her boyfriend.'

Jennifer cringed. 'And there's another one.'

Tom, who had reached down to pick up a dropped serving spoon, smiled. 'What was that?'

'Oh, nothing. Kids being kids.'

Angela clapped her hands together. 'Okay, everyone.

For today's lesson, we're going to make caramel shortcake. How does that sound?'

THE WIND HAD GOT UP, and the flurries of falling leaves were heavier than ever as Jennifer made her way back through Sycamore Park just after six o'clock. The sun was low in the sky, about to dip below the horizon. The clocks didn't go back for another couple of weeks—on Halloween this year—so she tried to enjoy the last few days of light she would have walking home. With the park getting a little spooky after dark, and with the cold drawing in, she would probably revert back to driving to and from work, and saving Sycamore Park for Bonky's walks on Saturday mornings.

She sighed. Just six weeks she had lived in Brentwell, yet already she felt she had lived a lifetime since leaving Mark. She had friends, responsibilities, even a potential boyfriend if she could just pluck up the courage to agree to one of Tom's frequent invitations. She felt part of a web, a string that if plucked would make a resonance, leaving an impression on the others. In her years with Mark she had been a piece of driftwood floating just below the surface of a lonely lake, invisible to everyone.

The Oak Leaf Café was closed, Angela having begun to shorten her hours for the coming winter. In November she would shorten even further, closing at 4 p.m., then from December to January she would open only at week-ends and for a couple of lunchtimes per week. Some years, she had told Jennifer, she shut entirely over January and February, and went off travelling somewhere. With many of the trees now turning skeletal, everything had the air of settling down for the winter.

To Jennifer's surprise, a light glowed through the frosted window in the door of Tom's shack. She found her heart thumping with nerves as she went over and knocked, wondering what had kept Tom so late.

'It's me,' she said.

'Come on in,' came Tom's cheerful reply.

Jennifer found him hunkered over a table against one ramshackle wall, an electric heater at his feet, a lamp bent over a piece of paper.

'What are you doing?' Jennifer asked.

'Come and have a look at this,' he said. 'I'm useless with words.'

He grabbed a chair for her and set it next to his.

'So, you decided to do it after all?'

Judging by the number of discarded attempts scattered across the table, Tom was on the tenth or eleventh attempt to create a handwritten flyer for his forthcoming acting class.

'The library said I could use a room on the upstairs floor every Thursday night,' Tom said. 'I decided it would be free, but each attendee should make an anonymous donation to the upkeep of Sycamore Park.' He frowned, giving the end of the pencil a little nibble.

'Uh, don't do that!' Jennifer grinned and gave his hand a little tap. 'You're like one of my kids.'

'Sorry … Miss,' Tom said. 'Seriously, I'm terrible with words. Can you tell me how to make this compelling? "Acting Class at 6 p.m. in the Library on Thursdays" doesn't really cut it.'

Jennifer picked up a couple of the drafts. 'You've made some good starts,' she said. 'Don't you have a computer or something, so that you don't waste so many trees?'

Tom arched an eyebrow. 'I prefer the personal touch,'

he said. 'What would you need to read to join up to this class?'

Jennifer couldn't help but feel a little flutter at the earnestness of his request. She couldn't recall Mark ever asking for her opinion on anything. Not one single time.

'Well, you need a hook, and something about yourself to draw people in,' she said. 'How about "Pay up for that motor," Acting Classes, with former *EastEnders* star Tom Reynolds.'

'I was in three episodes, and I didn't even have a named part.'

'They don't need to know that until they're in the door. Then you can charm them with your Thespian wit.'

'But isn't that a little misleading?'

Jennifer rolled her eyes. 'How about "former *EastEnders* actor" then?'

'That should work. Do you think it's fair to ask for donations?'

'Of course it is. They're getting an acting class with a professional, aren't they? And it's not like you're asking them to give up their life's savings. Just a pound or two here and there to help out the park.'

'The council budget for the next two years is likely to get blown on repairing the courtyard,' Tom said. 'I need new fence posts for the western edge of the duck pond, where the riverbank drops off too sharply.'

Jennifer smiled. 'I'm sure they'd understand.'

Tom frowned. He made to chew his pencil again before pulling it away at the last moment. 'If someone gives me the words to say, I can bring them to life,' Tom said, shaking his head. 'But getting the words … I'm useless.'

Jennifer patted him on the shoulder. 'You're doing a great job. Don't give up. By the way, have you eaten yet?'

Tom looked up. 'No … not yet. Um, you're not asking me out, are you?'

Jennifer felt a flush of heat. 'Uh, I'm asking you outside of this room,' she said. 'Unless you have a stash of food hidden away?'

'One of your kids left their lunchbox behind this afternoon,' Tom said. 'But I'm afraid I already passed it to Angela to give to Greg at their cooking class tonight.' He grinned. 'I did have a poke around inside, but apart from a half-eaten apple, there wasn't much to salvage.'

'So I guess it's a takeaway then?'

'At yours? I imagine the cat will be pleased to see me. Have you walked Bonky yet?'

Jennifer grimaced. 'Not yet. He'll be going stir-crazy by now.'

'Well, let's deal with that and then see what we can find.'

'Sounds good.'

'I can finish this tomorrow. Ah, one more thing.'

'What is it?'

'I, ah, don't have a phone. Is there any chance I can put your phone number down?'

'Am I likely to get bombarded with pseudo-auditions over the phone?'

'You might. Acting types can be a bit oddball.'

Jennifer grinned. 'I tell you what. I'll let you use my phone number if you help me with my lines for the teachers' drama. I only have five, but I still want them to sound good.'

'That's more than I had in *EastEnders*.' Tom grinned. 'Sure. What are you playing?'

'I'm a talking rabbit minstrel who instructs a wayward prince on the best way to live his life.' She lifted her hands to make mock rabbit ears. 'Why did you step on my tail? It might be fluffy, but it's not a marshmallow.'

'That's what you have to say? Seriously?'

Jennifer shrugged. 'Something like that.'

Tom laughed and tapped the piece of paper. 'You should sign up for my acting school. You could be my first customer.'

'Sure, why not? It'll be fun.'

'Great.' Tom let out a long breath, then smiled. 'Thanks so much for helping me. I really couldn't have done this without you.'

Jennifer smiled on the outside, but on the inside, a warm feeling was spreading through her body, even though the heater was turned a little too low to completely banish the chill.

'My pleasure,' she said.

29

APPRECIATION

'WOW, JULIUS LOOKS STERN TODAY,' Amy said, whispering behind Jennifer's desk at Rick, who was sipping coffee from a mug which read Brentwell Primary Harvest Festival on the side in letters designed to look like bundles of straw.

'I think he's plucked his eyebrows,' Rick said. 'Did you remember to do yours, Amy?' He smirked. 'There'll be armies of desperate single fathers at the festival.'

Amy gave her eyebrows an involuntary rub as Jennifer mouthed, 'He called you Amy.' Amy's response was to drop a pencil sharpener on the floor, the little attached box for the clippings popping out like a fleeing mouse to hide somewhere under Jennifer's desk. As Amy scrabbled for it, Downton stood up and clapped his hands together.

'Right, last word and then I'll leave you to get on with it. Looks like we're warm and dry for tomorrow, thank God. We're setting up the stalls tonight, so don't forget to come by Sycamore Park and help out. I have ah, an um, friend who said there'd be coffee and donuts for anyone who shows up.'

'Your friend's name is Tesco Metro, is it?' Old Don quipped. 'I've heard she's a right looker.'

Downton ignored him. 'And tomorrow morning the festival starts at 9 a.m. sharp. Have all your pupils there by eight if possible, and don't forget there are two buses leaving from the school at eight thirty for those who can't get there directly. Okay, that's it. I trust you're all ready?'

'Car's loaded with merch,' Rick said. 'Feels like I'm off on tour.'

'Butlins?' Jennifer said.

'In your dreams,' Rick said, rolling his eyes.

'Are you bringing your mother?'

Rick frowned. 'What, to Butlins?'

'The festival, you moron. Although I imagine she'd enjoy that too. You should get her out of the house from time to time.'

'Does your mother live in Brentwell?' Amy said, brushing bits of pencil sharpener clippings into a bin. 'You should ask her to come along.'

Rick glared at Jennifer, then shrugged. 'I'll think about it.'

At the front, Downton had been saying something about bringing raincoats, just in case. He clapped his hands together again. 'All right, let's do this. Fingers crossed it's not a complete disaster.'

'OKAY, Miss, you can come in now.'

Gavin, standing with his arms across the door, stepped back for Jennifer to enter. As she walked into the room, the kids all jumped up from their desks and began to cheer. Hanging across the middle of the classroom, the children had hung up a huge crepe paper banner. Written in slightly wonky painted letters was

Miss Steven – the best teacher ever!!!

'That's … wonderful.'

She took a step closer, noticing that someone had drawn in the missing S with felt tip pen.

'Miss, we just wanted to say that you're the best teacher ever,' Gavin said, beaming.

'I gathered that. Thank you.'

She wiped away a tear. From somewhere near the back came a snigger, followed by 'She's crying.'

'Are you … ready … for tomorrow?'

'Look, Miss.'

Gavin waved behind her. She turned. On her desk dozens of plastic containers stood in unsteady towers. She grabbed a couple of the more unstable and moved them to safer ground, then plucked off a couple of lids to have a look at the contents.

The aromas of maple, cinnamon, chocolate, ginger, walnut, and a dozen others made her close her eyes with delight.

'We're pretty sure Paul's one's got poison in it, but we can't remember which one it is,' Gavin said. 'We'll have to keep an eye out for anyone dying.'

'It's the lemon cake,' Matthew said suddenly, making Jennifer blink with surprise as the other kids laughed. It felt almost like a novelty that she would have to reprimand Matthew for bullying.

'Shut up and eat your Hob Knobs,' Paul retorted, some in-joke that went right over Jennifer's head as the other kids began to laugh, even, to her relief, Matthew.

Jennifer moved a couple of pots aside so that she had

room for her own bag, overloaded with its contents this morning.

'Okay, so the bad news is that we're not allowed to eat any of these cakes until tomorrow—because, you know, we have to sell them—and the other bad news is that I haven't got anything nearly as good, but Mr. Downton has authorised us to have a little class party, since you've all done such a good job.'

The kids cheered as Jennifer began to unload the contents of her bag: a dozen packets of biscuits, chocolates, and crisps from the supermarket, together with a pack of paper plates with maple-leaf designs.

'No way, she's got Coke!'

'If anyone's parents want to complain that I'm ruining your teeth, please tell them to call the school office and ask for Mr. Downton,' Jennifer said, as eager fingers began to rip bags open, their contents spraying like confetti around the classroom. 'And please try not to drop anything on the floor.'

'Miss Stevens,' Downton said, coming to stand over her desk with an imposing frown on his face. 'Is there any chance you could put your phone on silent when you leave it on your desk? If I hear Gloria Gaynor sing *I Will Survive* one more time, I think I'll top myself. Have you been putting your phone number into dodgy internet sites again?'

'Sorry, sir,' Jennifer said, giving him a smile that melted his frown just a little.

'At least put it in your bag.'

As Downton went back to his own desk, Jennifer opened her phone. Nine missed calls, all from the same number. It wasn't one she recognised, but the caller had left a voicemail on one occasion, so Jennifer pressed the play option and held the phone to her ear.

'Hello?' came a familiar voice. 'Is this the number to sign up for acting classes with former *EastEnders* actor Tom Reynolds? If you have places left, I'd really like to reserve one. I'm happy to donate whatever you want. My name is Regina Clover.'

Jennifer smiled. They'd only put the posters for Tom's class up yesterday, and he had a customer already.

She couldn't wait to see the smile on his face when they met for a pre-harvest festival dinner tonight.

30

FESTIVITIES

THE SUN WAS JUST PEEKING above the rooftops, bringing with it a mid-autumn warmth that had got James excited enough to jump down from the bed, march proudly across the floor through the shards of sunlight allowed in by the curtains, then resume his sentry position on the window ledge. Bonky, perhaps anticipating that today was a special day, was already bouncing around the room, ready to get going.

Jennifer jumped out of bed and hurried to get ready, aware that she was supposed to be at the park in advance of any of her class arriving. Bonky, perhaps aware he was going to be getting an extended walk—Angela had offered to provide a basket at the café should he get tired from all the attention the kids were likely to give him—was scratching at the door, keen to get outside.

She was just about to open the door when the buzzer rang. She pressed the button on the intercom beside the door, and a picture of Tom appeared on the screen. Jennifer smiled as she pressed the release button to open the downstairs door. A few seconds later, the sound of foot-steps came from outside, followed by a light knock.

'I got coffees from the café up the street,' Tom said, holding up two paper cups as Jennifer let him inside.

'You're a legend. Thanks so much for helping me, and I'm so sorry about yesterday.'

Tom laughed. 'Oh, fixing the awnings? That's what park caretakers are for.'

'I don't think Downton planned for the wind.'

'It can really gust at this time of year. I just went over to check though, and they're all still there.'

'That's great. I'm also sorry about cancelling dinner yesterday. I was so tired.'

Tom shrugged. 'It's okay. I went home, lay on the sofa and cried for a few hours. It wasn't too bad.'

'I'll make it up to you.'

'There's nothing to make up. You've helped me out more than you know. Especially with the acting class.' He grimaced. 'I can't wait for next week.'

'Ha, don't worry, Regina won't be alone. Jennifer held up her phone. 'I've had three more calls. What are you planning to teach in your first class?'

Tom grinned. 'How to sell a motor to Phil Mitchell.'

'Really? Then I'd better make sure I leave room in my schedule.'

'You won't want to miss it.'

Tom handed Jennifer a coffee, then set his own down on Jennifer's kitchen table. He nodded towards the window ledge, where James was staring at him with murderous intent.

'Um, do I have time to stroke the cat for five minutes?' he said.

'Just five minutes. Then we're loading.'

With James's feline needs sorted and the coffees drunk,

they got to work. Beside the door were a stack of boxes containing cakes for sale on Jennifer's class's stall. The kids were bringing more, but she had needed to take home all those brought to school yesterday. Her flat had been filled with a tantalizing mixture of aromas ever since. Some of them were at Angela's level of skill, and it had taken all Jennifer's willpower not to try a couple of small samples.

Tom had brought his car, because it was a little bigger than Jennifer's and had room for all the boxes. As soon as they were loaded, Jennifer climbed into the passenger seat, Bonky jumped up on her lap, and they headed for Sycamore Park.

It was still only eight o'clock but several teachers had already shown up, and a few kids were running about on the grass while their parents stood in groups, hands in pockets, hopping from foot to foot as the morning cold gradually gave way with the sun appearing above the trees. Jennifer and Tom had just begun unloading when she saw Greg coming out of the Oak Leaf Café with one of Angela's maple lattes in his hands. He gave her a sour nod as she waved.

In the courtyard, the stalls had been set up in a semi-circle along freshly laid paving stones. Streamers hung from Big Gerry's lower branches, and a buzz of excitement filled the air. Jennifer had been focused on her class's cake stall for weeks, but now she found herself excited to see other stalls and activities, including craft goods, drinks, sandwiches and pies, shooting galleries, skittles, even a hit-the-weasel game. A rather unseasonable maypole had been set up in the courtyard's centre, its central pillar encircled by fluttering streamers in shades of oranges, reds, and browns.

On the far side of the courtyard, a small stage had been set up. In addition to the teachers' drama, a couple of local folk bands were going to play, and a few dance groups would also perform. A pretty backdrop showing a harvested field filled with bales of hay had been painted and hung up behind it.

Amy was standing in front of the stage, in between the stage itself and the first of a few lines of wooden benches, looking frantic. Having finished unloading the boxes of cakes and left them for Gavin's eager team to arrange, Jennifer wandered over.

'What's up? You don't look so excited.'

Amy stared at her, blinking wildly like a shocked deer.

'We have a crisis,' she said. 'Oh my. I don't think we're going to be able to pull this off. We'll have to cancel.'

'Why? What's up?'

'Karen Jenkins pulled out.'

'The school nurse? Why?'

'She's got influenza. We're a character down.'

Jennifer glanced over her shoulder at Tom, who was talking amicably with a group of parents.

'My, uh, friend, he's a bit of an actor,' Jennifer said. 'I'm sure he could fill in. Karen only had a few lines, didn't she?'

'Yeah, but she was the princess. And she has to … you know.'

Jennifer gave a slow nod. She glanced around the crowd, then turned back to Amy, trying to look dramatic. 'You,' she said, making a point of sounding grave. 'I know how dedicated you've been to this play. Don't pretend you haven't memorised the entire script.'

'Well, yes, kind of—'

'Then you'll have to step up from your role to Karen's. What were you?'

'A jester.'

Jennifer nodded. 'I'll ask Tom if he can take over your part. And you can take Karen's.'

'But what about … what about…?'

Jennifer patted Amy on the shoulder. 'Don't worry. It'll be all right. Sometimes we have to do what needs to be done, don't we?'

Amy took a deep breath. 'We do. I just hope Rick will understand.'

'I'm sure he will. Do you have a copy of the script I could show Tom?'

'I'll hunt one out.'

Jennifer headed over to her stall, where her class management team were hard at work setting everything up. Gavin, holding a clipboard which appeared to be for show as it had nothing clipped to it, was marshalling Paul Lemon in arranging the cakes on the table, while the Jarder twins were slicing them into saleable pieces. Matthew was following them around, sticking price labels in beautiful cursive handwriting on to each plate.

They were nearly done when Gavin held up a plastic box. 'Good work, guys. Now, one slice of each goes into this box for Matt's mum, since she can't be here.'

'Mate, you don't have to.'

'Yeah, we do. Except Paul's mum's lemon cake. We want your mum to get well not get worse.'

'Shut up, it's not that bad!'

Gavin snorted. 'All right, perhaps just a thin slice.'

'You really don't have to.'

'Mate, don't worry, if she can't eat it all, you get it, don't you? Plus, it's a mind trick, isn't it? That's what my dad reckons. When people see a bit missing, they'll think that cake's popular. Don't worry, Paul, we can just put a lump of your mum's cake in the bin, then hopefully we can sell the rest of it.'

'Ha ha,' Paul said, rolling his eyes. 'Is that trick like if you wish Argyle might win, then eventually, in a hundred years or so, they might?'

'Shut up, Lemons.'

'Yeah, shut up, Lemons,' Matthew added. 'We've got Doncaster this afternoon. Five nil, easy.' He turned to Gavin. 'Is your dad still going?'

'Nah. He's coming here, isn't he? He reckoned he's lent his season ticket to some homeless guy or something.'

'Isn't the guy suffering enough?' Paul said with a loud chortle. 'Might as well steal his blanket while you're at it.'

Gavin grinned. 'I think a pigeon just took a dump on your mum's cake.'

'That's a melted chocolate drop.'

'Whatever.'

'All going well, is it?' Jennifer said.

'Yes, Miss.'

'Yes, Miss.'

'Yes, Miss.'

The Jarder twins were too busy fussing over Bonky to say anything.

'Well, it looks great,' Jennifer said. 'You've done a wonderful job.'

'Thanks, Miss.'

'Thanks, Miss.'

'Thanks, Miss.'

Jennifer wandered over to the courtyard's edge, where Greg Downton was talking to Amy while Don Jones and Colin Tiller, both with their hands stuffed into their pockets, stood either side of him.

'Well,' Downton said as Jennifer came into earshot. 'Now's your chance to ask him.'

Downton nodded towards the northern park entrance just past the Oak Leaf Café where Angela was arranging salt and pepper pots on the outdoor tables. A man in a sweatshirt with the hood pulled over his head was pushing an older woman in a wheelchair. The woman had a basket on her lap as though she meant to fill it with cakes, and a wide grin on her face.

'Is that … who is that?' Amy said, frowning at Jennifer.

'Are you ready for the big reveal?'

'What reveal?'

Jennifer cupped her hands around her mouth. 'Good morning, Rick!' she called.

Rick looked up, his face just visible inside the hood he had pulled tight with a drawstring.

Amy clutched Jennifer's arm so tightly Jennifer nearly fell. 'Oh, my. Is he married? Is that his wife? She's not what I would have expected. She's so old, and you know, disabled—'

'That's his mother, Amy.'

As Rick, still hiding inside the hood, pushed the wheelchair to a stop beneath Big Gerry's leaning branches, Jennifer called, 'Good morning, Mrs. Fellow!'

'Oh, good morning, dear. Eric, are you going to introduce me to your friends?'

'It's colleagues, Mother. None of these people are my friends.'

'It was one and the same in my day, Eric.'

Amy pulled Jennifer close. 'What's this "Eric" business?'

'That's his name.'

'But … oh, I get it.' Amy let out a guffaw. 'Eric … Rick. Eric … Rick.'

With a sigh, Rick loosened the drawstrings and pushed the hood back. 'Please, Amy. Don't make this any harder.'

'There you are, Eric,' Downton said, giving Jennifer and Amy a quick smirk. 'About time. Why don't you go and marshal your class before there's complete anarchy, while in the meantime I'll take your lovely mother over to that delightful café over there for a wonderful coffee.'

Rick, refusing to look at Downton, twitched in a way that could be perceived as a nod. 'Sure.'

As Rick headed off to his class's stall, Jennifer turned to Amy. 'Isn't this just a wonderful day?'

By FIVE TO TEN, the courtyard was teeming with people. The kids were all in position around their stalls, the first band was ready on the stage to play, and even Rick seemed to have cheered up. Jennifer said good morning to Marlie Gordon, who introduced Jennifer to John Gordon, Gavin's dad. While there might not have been a ring on either of their fingers, that they were chatting amicably boded well for Gavin and his ongoing behavioural shift.

'Jennifer? Have you got a sec?'

Jennifer turned to see Amy standing behind her with an older lady at her shoulder. She had kind eyes and a warm smile. The sun, shining through the trees seemed to light up her face.

'This is Clara,' Amy said. 'Clara Goldsmith.' Just in case the penny took a moment to drop, she added, 'Your predecessor.'

'Lovely to meet you, dear,' Clara said. 'I was just chatting to a few of my old lot over there, and I have to say, it sounds like you've made a good impression. And how on earth did you get Gavin and Matthew to be such good friends?'

Jennifer smiled. 'Complete luck. Thank you for coming. It's lovely to meet you at last.'

Clara nodded. 'I'd tell you to give me a call if you have

any problems, but I'm retired and happy to stay that way. However, I wouldn't mind a slice of cake or two.'

'Ask Gavin to give you a discount. Tell him I said.'

Clara chuckled. 'Oh, he'd never believe me, the little so-and-so.'

'Will you be sticking around for the play?' Amy said.

'I wouldn't miss it for the world,' Clara said. 'Who's playing the prince?'

'Rick,' Jennifer said.

Clara chuckled again and rolled her eyes. 'How surprising. Well, I hope whoever's unlucky enough to be the princess escapes with nothing more than a peck on the cheek.' As Amy, eyes wide, went bright red, Clara nudged Jennifer and added, 'If it was me, I'd have given the part to Moody Maud. That would have shown him.'

Up on the stage, Downton banged a spoon against a frying pan and called for quiet. Clara said goodbye to Jennifer and moved back through the crowd. As Jennifer stood next to Amy, she glanced across the assembled crowd and spotted Matthew Bridges' dad, holding up an iPad so that someone on the screen could see what was going on.

'All right, everyone,' Downton said, taking hold of the microphone and looking no less awkward than he did when they had a meeting at school, 'Ah, thanks for coming and all that. I'd just like to give a big shout of thanks to everyone on the staff—and the kids, of course—for all your hard work. I'm quite amazed that you managed to pull it off. At this point last year I think we'd had a couple of stalls collapse and at least two kids go missing, so small mercies, really. Then there was that beehive some dog disturbed … but there's no need to bring that up.' He gave a big, humourless smile. 'And I'd like to give a special thanks to the council for not cutting down that big tree over there. Even though it looks like it might be about to collapse anyway, I'm told it's been here quite a while. I wouldn't suggest standing right underneath it, though, just in case.'

A cheer went up from the crowd, as well as a couple of shouts to hurry up. Jennifer twisted as someone grabbed her arm, and she turned to see Angela with tears in her eyes.

'Oh, my gosh ... he's so funny,' she said, barely able to speak.

Jennifer shook her head. 'I think you're putting a bit too much sugar in your coffee,' she said.

'So, anyway, to officially open the harvest festival— something I realised we'd overlooked until last night—I'd like you to give a warm welcome to Brentwell's very own she-devil with a thawed heart, Regina Clover.'

To lukewarm applause and a few sly boos, Regina Clover, beaming in a straw hat that looked straight out of Downton's wardrobe, climbed up on to the stage and walked over to the microphone, waving to the crowd as she did so, seemingly oblivious to the grumbles being passed around.

'Such a fine day, such a fine day,' she said, giving a tittering laugh. 'How lovely to see so many of you. Just in case you're unaware, there's a council by-election next month.' She winked. 'Not to try and nudge you, or anything....'

Jennifer found Tom standing beside her. 'I'm not sure she needs acting lessons,' he said, leaning close. 'I think she could teach me a thing or two.'

'...and so, at least until the council has no other choice but to call in the bulldozers—' Regina slapped her thigh and giggled, '—I'd like to welcome you to Sycamore Park on this fine October day, and declare the Brentwell Primary School Harvest Festival officially ... open!'

Cheers went up from the crowd, as well as a few sighs of relief. The band began to play, and parents flocked towards the stalls to try out cakes and sandwiches, juices and coffees, to buy vegetables, fruits, and craft goods, and to try their hand at a dozen different games. Jennifer looked up at Tom. With the sun just behind his face, he looked incredibly handsome, and when he smiled at her, she felt a sense of warmth that defied the chilly wind that had a habit of blowing through the trees, and she realised that on this day, in the middle of this park, in this little town, she felt truly and completely alive.

'My hands are cold,' she said.

'What? I think I have some gloves here somewhere—'

'No. Specifically my left hand. The one closest to your right hand.'

'Oh.'

Jennifer watched him. His smile dropped a little, but his eyes watched hers with great intensity. The chilly wind that had been riffling her hair was suddenly hidden beneath the warmth of Tom's fingers.

'So, uh, can we have that date tonight at long last?' Tom said.

'I think we can.'

'That's good.' Tom continued to look at her. He smiled again. 'Um … would it be permissible for me to kiss you in front of your pupils?' Tom asked, giving Jennifer a shy smile.

Jennifer felt a lump in her throat, but with a scowl, shook her head. 'No, it absolutely would not,' she said, grinning. Then, in a voice she hoped was loud enough for him to hear over the hammering drumbeat of her heart, she said, 'However, I'd be happy to let you kiss me later, after they've all gone home.'

Tom's cheeks appeared to redden, but of course, it

could have just been the cold. 'Thanks. I'm looking forward to it.'

Jennifer would have been happy to stay in this position, staring into Tom's eyes, for at least the next week, but a sudden voice rose over the crowd:

'Miss! Miss! Quick, Paul dropped that swot Vickers' mum's chocolate cake on the grass!'

Jennifer rolled her eyes, then adopted her best teacher expression as she turned around to find Gavin pushing through the crowd towards her, a chocolate cake held in his hands, bits of grass sticking out of a slightly flattened top.

'Well, quickly, pick the grass out of it and get it back on the stall for sale. Haven't you heard of the three-second rule?'

Gavin nodded. 'Got it, Miss.'

'Good lad.'

Tom laughed. 'A bit of nature never hurt anyone,' he said. Then, spotting someone he knew through the crowd, he added, 'I'll be back in a minute. Will you be right here or will I have to put on my hat and stalk you?'

Jennifer looked down at Bonky, bouncing around her feet. 'I think I'll go and find somewhere a little warmer for this one for a while,' she said. 'I'll see you in a minute?'

'And the minute after that, and the one after that,' Tom said.

Jennifer's heart was still fluttering. 'Okay.'

Reluctantly, she left Tom behind, heading through the crowd to the Oak Leaf Café. The sign on the front door had been turned around to closed, even though there were several customers sitting at the tables outside. Jennifer frowned, looking around her. There was no sign of Angela, but as she glanced back at the window, she caught sight of movement inside.

'Let's have a look,' she said, scooping Bonky up into her arms. 'Let's see if she's in there.'

As soon as she pressed her face to the window, however, she wished she hadn't. Angela was standing in the middle of the restaurant, holding the hands of Greg Downton, who stood facing her. Then, as Jennifer stared, Downton bent down as Angela stood up on tiptoes, and they shared the most romantic kiss Jennifer had ever seen outside of a Saturday afternoon classic movie.

'Ah, I guess you're going under my jacket if you're cold,' she said to Bonky, pulling away before either Angela or Downton could see her. 'Come on. We have to find Tom. Right now.'

He was talking to Pete Markham and a man Jennifer recognised as the council worker she had spoken to last week. He looked round as she approached, stepping aside as though to draw her into his circle, but Jennifer just grabbed his arm and pulled him close.

'I need a word. Right now.'

'Oh, sure. What's up?'

Jennifer shook her head. 'Not here.' She glanced around, looking for a suitable place. 'Behind Big Gerry.'

'Right. Okay.'

She smiled to Pete and the man from the council, then took Tom's hand and pulled him after her. Despite Big Gerry's girth, they weren't entirely hidden, but as long as no one from her class decided to look behind the stalls during the next couple of minutes, she was sure she would just about get away with it.

'What's up?' Tom said.

'I'm not being left out,' she said.

'Of what?'

'I just saw Angela and Downton in the Oak Leaf Café. And in about half an hour, my wonderful colleague Rick is going to get a surprise from his newly anointed princess. Now is my turn.'

'For what … *oh.*'

'Now,' Jennifer said. 'Now's the exact right time. As long as Big Gerry doesn't choose this exact moment to fall down.'

Tom lifted his eyebrows. 'But … your stall is right there.'

'I don't care. Quickly.'

Bonky whined as Jennifer squeezed him between herself and Tom.

'The cat will be jealous,' Tom said, but his voice had quietened as he leaned close.

'You can make it up to him later,' Jennifer said, closing her eyes, taking Tom's hands, and pulling him close, closer, closest, as the wind rustled through the branches overhead, someone cheered, and somewhere else, Jennifer felt a piece of her broken heart fitting back into place.

Acknowledgements

Many thanks goes to Elizabeth Mackey for the cover, Jenny Avery for your endless wisdom, Paige for the editorial stuff, and also to my eternal muses Jenny Twist and John Daulton, whose words of encouragement got me where I am today, nearly ten years after the journey started.

Lastly, but certainly not least, many thanks goes to my wonderful Patreon supporters:

Carl Rod, Rosemary Kenny, Jane Ornelas, Ron, Betty Martin, Gail Beth Le Vine, Anja Peerdeman, Sharon Kenneson, Jennie Brown, Leigh McEwan, Amaranth Dawe, Janet Hodgson, and Katherine Crispin

and to everyone's who's bought me a coffee recently:

Mariane, Denise, Janet, Christine, and a couple of anonymous readers

You guys are fantastic and your support means so much.

For more information:
www.amillionmilesfromanywhere.net

Printed in Great Britain
by Amazon